AFTER THE WAR IS OVER

Robinson felt cold at meeting that too-steady gaze. He whispered shakily, 'Is it – bad?'

'The worst. Physically the country's recovering. But biologically, we've reached a crossroads and taken the wrong fork.'

'What do you mean? *What do you mean?*'

Drummond let him have it then. 'The birth rate's a little over half the prewar,' he said, 'and about seventy-five percent of all births are mutant, and it's everywhere. There are no safe places . . . We have to decide what to do about it. And soon. It's wrecking our civilization. People are going crazy as birth after birth is monstrous.'

Robinson straightened in his chair. 'Yes. Yes, we'll have to act fast. We're mobilized,' he said. 'We have the men and the weapons and the organization. They won't be able to resist.'

Drummond felt a swift and horrible wrenching of fear. 'What are you getting at?'

'Racial deat'   'o be
sterilized wl

D1514178

Also by Poul Anderson in Sphere Books:

THREE WORLDS TO CONQUER
THE PEOPLE OF THE WIND
THE AVATAR
MIRKHEIM
A KNIGHT OF GHOSTS AND SHADOWS
THE DANCER FROM ATLANTIS
A CIRCUS OF HELLS
THERE WILL BE TIME

Twilight World

POUL ANDERSON

SPHERE BOOKS LIMITED
London and Sydney

First published in Great Britain by
Sphere Books Ltd 1984
30–32 Gray's Inn Road, London WC1X 8JL
Copyright © 1981 by Poul Anderson
First published in the United States of America by
Tor Books 1983

This is a work of fiction. All the characters and events
portrayed in this book are fictional, and any resemblance to
real people or incidents is purely coincidental.

TRADE
MARK

This book is sold subject to the condition that
is shall not, by way of trade or otherwise, be lent,
re-sold, hired out or otherwise circulated without
the publisher's prior consent in any form of
binding or cover other than that in which it is
published and without a similar condition
including this condition being imposed on the
subsequent purchaser.

Set in 9½/11 pt Compugraphic Plantin

Printed and bound in Great Britain by
Collins, Glasgow.

To John W. Campbell, Jr.

Twilight World

Prologue

On the world's loom
Weave the Norns doom,
Nor may they guide it nor change.

– Wagner: *Siegfried*

1

Ten miles up, it hardly showed. Earth was a cloudy green and brown blur, the vault of the stratosphere reaching changelessly out to infinity, and beyond the pulsing engine there was silence and serenity no man could ever touch. Looking down, Hugh Drummond could see the Mississippi gleaming like a dream sword, and its slow curve matched the contours on his map. The hills, the sea, the sun and wind and rain, they didn't change. Not in less than a million slow-striding years, and humankind was too brief a flicker for that.

Farther down, though, and especially where cities had been –

The man in the stratojet swore softly and bitterly, his knuckles whitening on the controls. He was a big man, his gaunt rangy form sprawling awkwardly in the tiny pressure cabin, and he wasn't quite forty. But his dark hair was streaked with gray, his shoulders stooped in the shabby flying suit, and his long homely face was drawn into haggard lines. The eyes were black-rimmed and sunken with weariness, something dreadful about their intensity. He had seen too much, survived too much, until he began to look like most other people of the world. *Heir of the ages*, he thought dully.

Mechanically, he went through the motions of following his course. Natural landmarks were still there, and he had powerful binoculars to help him. But he didn't use them much. They showed too many broad shallow craters, whose vitreous smoothness threw back sunlight with the flat blank glitter of a snake's eye, and the churned and blasted desolation of ground about them. And the region of total deadness was worse: twisted leafless trees, blowing sand, tumbled skeletons, perhaps at night a baleful blue glow of fluorescence. The bombs had been nightmare, riding in on wings of fire and horror to shake the planet with the death of cities.

But the radioactive dust was more than nightmare.

He passed over villages and small towns. Some of them were deserted, the dust or plague or economic breakdown making them untenable. Others still seemed to be feebly alive. Especially in the Middle West, there was a pathetic struggle to return to agriculture, but the insects and blights –

Drummond shrugged. After nearly two years of this, over the scarred and maimed planet, he should be used to it. The United States had been lucky. Europe, now –

Der Untergang des Abendlandes, he thought grayly. *Spengler and the rest foresaw the collapse of a topheavy civilization. They didn't foresee atomic bombs, radioactive-dust bombs, bacteria bombs, blight bombs – the bombs flying like senseless insects over a shivering world. So they didn't guess what the collapse would really mean.*

Deliberately, he pushed the thought out of his conscious mind. He didn't want to dwell on it. He'd lived with it two years, and that was two eternities too long. And anyway, he was nearly home now.

The capital of the United States was below him, and he sent the stratojet slanting down in a long thunderous dive toward the mountains. Not much of a capital, the little town huddled on a slope of the Cascades, but the waters of the Potomac had filled the grave of Washington. Strictly speaking, there was no nucleus of government yet; surviving officialdom was scattered over the country, keeping in precarious touch by plane and radio. But Taylor, Oregon, came as close to being the nerve center as any other place.

He gave the signal on the transmitter, knowing with a faint crawl along his spine of the rocket batteries trained on him from the green of those mountains. When one plane could carry the end of a city, all planes were under suspicion. Not that anyone outside was supposed to know that that innocuous little town was important. But you never could tell. The war wasn't officially over. It might never be, with sheer personal survival overriding the urgency of treaties.

A tight-beam transmitter gave him a cautious: 'Okay. Can you land in the street?'

It was a narrow, dusty track between two rows of wooden houses, but Drummond was a good pilot and this was a good jet. 'Yeah,' he said. His voice had grown unused to speech.

He cut speed in a spiral descent until he was gliding with only the faintest whisper of wind across his ship. Touching wheels to the street, he slammed on the brake and bounced to a halt.

Silence struck at him like a physical blow. The engine stilled, the sun beating down from a brassy sky on the drabness of rude 'temporary' dwellings, the total-seeming desertion beneath impassive mountains – Home! Hugh Drummond laughed, a short harsh bark with nothing of humor in it, and swung open the cockpit canopy.

There were actually quite a few people peering from doorways and side streets. They looked fairly well-fed and well-dressed, many in uniform, they seemed to have purpose and hope. But this, of course, was the capital of the United States of America, the world's most fortunate country.

'Get out – quick!'

The peremptory voice roused Drummond from the introspection which lonely months had made habitual. He looked down at a gang of men in mechanics' outfits, led by a harassed-looking man in captain's uniform. 'Oh – of course,' he said slowly. 'You want to hide the jet. And, naturally, a regular landing field would give you away.'

'Hurry, get out, you infernal idiot! Anyone, *anyone* might come over and see you.'

'They wouldn't get unnoticed past an efficient detection system, and you still have that,' said Drummond, sliding his booted legs over the cockpit edge. 'And anyway, there won't be any more raids. The war's over.'

'Wish I could believe that, but who're you to say? Get a move on!'

The mechs hustled the jet down the street. Drummond watched it go with an odd feeling of loneliness. After all, it had been his home for – how long?

The machine was stopped before a false house whose entire front swung aside. A concrete ramp led downward, and Drummond could see a cavernous immensity below. Light within it gleamed off silvery rows of aircraft.

'Pretty neat,' he admitted. 'Not that it matters any more. Probably it never did. Most of the hell came over on robot rockets. Oh, well.' He fished his pipe from his jacket. Colonel's insignia glittered briefly as the garment flipped back.

'Oh . . . sorry, sir!' exclaimed the captain. 'I didn't know –'

''S'okay. I've gotten out of the habit of wearing a regular uniform. A lot of places I've been, an American wouldn't be very popular.' Drummond stuffed tobacco into his briar, scowling. He hated to think how often he'd had to use the Colt at his hip, or even the machine guns in his jet, to save himself. He inhaled smoke gratefully. It seemed to drown out some of the bitter taste.

'General Robinson said to bring you to him when you arrived, sir,' said the captain. 'This way, please.'

They went down the street, their boots scuffing up little acrid clouds of dust. Drummond looked sharply about him. He'd left soon after the fighting – the two-month Ragnarok which had tapered off when the organization of both sides broke down too far to keep on making and sending the bombs and maintaining order with famine and pestilence starting their gallop across the homeland. At that time, the United States was a cityless, anarchic tumult, and he'd had only the briefest of radio exchanges since then, whenever he could get at a long-range set still in working order. They'd made remarkable progress meanwhile. How much, he didn't know, but the very existence of something like a capital was sufficient proof. General Robinson – Drummond's lined face twisted into a frown. He didn't know the man. He'd been expecting to be received by the President, who had sent him and some others out. Unless the others had – No, he was the only one who'd been in eastern Europe and western Asia. He was sure of that.

Two sentries guarded the entrance to what was obviously a converted general store. But there were no more stores. There was nothing to put in them. Drummond entered the cool dimness of an antechamber. The clatter of a typewriter, the Wac operating it – He blinked. It hardly seemed possible. Type-writers and secretaries – hadn't they gone out with the whole world, two years ago? If the Dark Ages had returned to Earth, it didn't seem – *right* – that there should still be typewriters. It didn't fit.

He saw that the captain had opened the inner door for him. As he stepped through, he grew aware how tired he was. When he saluted the man behind the desk, his arm weighed a ton.

'At ease, at ease.' Robinson's voice was genial. Despite the five stars on his shoulders, he wore no tie or coat, and his round face was smiling. Still, he looked tough and competent underneath. To run things nowadays, he'd have to be.

'Sit down, Colonel Drummond.' Robinson gestured to a chair near his own and the aviator collapsed into it, shivering. His haunted eyes roved the office. It was almost well enough out-fitted to be prewar.

Prewar! A word like a sword, cutting across history and hazing the past until it was a vague gold glow through drifting, red-shot smoke. And only two years. Only two years! Surely sanity was meaningless in a world of such nightmare inversions. Why, he could hardly remember Barbara and the kids. Their faces were drowned in a tide of others – starved faces, dead faces, human faces become beast-formed with want and pain and grinding hate. His grief was lost in the sorrow of a world, and in some ways he had become a machine himself.

'You look plenty tired,' said Robinson.

'Yeah . . . Yes, sir.'

'Skip the formality. I don't go in for it. We'll be working pretty close together, can't take time to be diplomatic.'

'Uh-huh. I came over the North Pole, you know, and turned west. Haven't slept since – Rough time. But, if I may ask you –' Drummond hesitated.

'I? I suppose I'm President. Ex-officio, pro tem, or something. Here, you need a drink.' Robinson got bottle and glasses from a drawer. The liquor gurgled out pungently. 'Ten-year-old Scotch. Till it gives out, I'm laying off my adjutant's bathtub brew. *Gambai*.' Drummond thought Robinson must have flown the Hump in World War Two to learn that toast. That would have been long ago, when he was young and it was still possible to win a war.

The fiery, smoky stuff jolted Drummond back toward wakefulness. Its glow was pleasant in his empty stomach. He heard Robinson's voice with a surrealistic sharpness:

'Yes, I'm at the head now. My predecessors made the mistake of sticking together, and of traveling a good deal in trying to pull the country back into shape. So I think the sickness got the President and the Cabinet, and I know it got several others. Of course, there was no way to hold an election. The armed forces had almost the only organization left, so we had to run things. Berger was in charge, but he shot himself when he learned he'd breathed radio-dust. Then the command fell to me. I've been lucky so far.'

'I see.' It didn't make much difference. A few dozen more deaths weren't much, out of all the nameless millions. 'Do you expect to – continue lucky?' A brutally blunt question, maybe, but words weren't bombs.

'I do.' Robinson was firm about that. 'We've learned by experience, learned a lot. We've scattered the army, broken it into small outposts at key points throughout the country. For quite a while, we stopped travel altogether except for absolute emergencies, and then only with elaborate precautions. That smothered the epidemics. The microbes were bred to work in crowded areas, you know. They were almost immune to known medical techniques, but without hosts and carriers they died. I guess natural bacteria ate up most of them. We still take care in traveling, but we're pretty safe now.'

'Did any of the others come back? There were a lot like me, sent out to see what really had happened to the world.'

'One did, from South America. Their situation is similar to ours, though they lacked our tight organization and have gone further toward anarchy. Nobody else returned but you.'

It wasn't surprising. In fact, it was cause for astonishment that anyone had come back. Drummond had volunteered after the bomb erasing St. Louis had taken his family, not expecting to survive and not caring much whether he did. Maybe that was why he had.

'You can take your time about writing a detailed report,' said Robinson, 'but in general, how are things over there?'

Drummond shrugged. 'The war's over. Burned out. Europe has gone back to savagery. They were caught between America and Asia, and the bombs came both ways; after distribution systems went, and blights took the crops, their overpopulation did the rest. Not many survivors, and they're starving animals. Russia, from what I saw, has managed something like you've done here, in about four different independent regions, though they're worse off than we. Naturally, I couldn't find out much there. I didn't get to India or China, but in Russia I heard rumors. No, the world's disintegrated too far to continue the war.'

'Then we can come out in the open,' said Robinson softly. 'We can really start rebuilding. I don't think there'll ever be another war, Drummond. I think the memory of this one is carved too deep for us ever to forget.'

'Can you shrug it off that easily?'

'No, no, of course not. Our culture hasn't lost its continuity, but it's had a terrific setback. We'll never wholly get over it. But – we're on our way up again.'

The general rose, glancing at his watch. '1800 hours. Come on, Drummond, let's get home.'

'Home?'

'Yes, you'll stay with me. Man, you look like the original zombie. You'll need a month or more of sleeping between clean sheets, home cooking and home atmosphere. My wife'll be glad to have you, we see almost no new faces. And as long as we work together, I'd like to keep you handy. The shortage of competent men is terrific.'

They went down the street, an aide following. Drummond was again conscious of the weariness aching in him. A home – after two years of ghost towns, of shattered chimneys above blood-dappled snow, of flimsy lean-tos housing starvation and death.

'Your jet'll be mighty useful too,' said Robinson. 'Those atomic-powered craft are scarcer than hens' teeth used to be.' He chuckled with a metallic note, as at a rather grim joke. 'Got you through all that time of flying without needing fuel. Any trouble, by the way?'

'Some, but there were enough spare parts to be found.' No need to tell of those frantic hours and days of slaving, desperate improvisation, hunger and plague stalking him who stayed over-long. He'd had his troubles getting food too, despite the plentiful supplies he started out with. He'd fought for scraps in the winters, beaten off maniacs who would have killed him for a bird he'd shot or a dead horse he'd scavenged or the meat on his own bones. He hated that plundering, and would not have cared personally if they managed to destroy him. But he had a mission, and the mission was all he had had left as a focal point in his life, so he had clung to it at any price.

And now the job was over, and he realized he could rest. He didn't dare. Rest would give him time to remember. Maybe he could find surcease in the gigantic work of reconstruction. Maybe.

'Here we are,' said Robinson.

Drummond blinked in new amazement. There was a car, camouflaged under trees, with a military chauffeur – a *car!* And in pretty fair shape, too.

'We're got a few oil wells going again, and a small patched-up refinery,' explained the general. 'It furnishes enough gas and oil for what official traffic we have.'

They got in the rear seat. The aide sat in front, a rifle across his knees. The car started down the mountain road.

'Where to?' asked Drummond a little dazedly.

Robinson smiled. 'Personally,' he said, 'I'm almost the only lucky man on Earth. We had a summer cottage on Lake Taylor, a few miles from here. My wife was there when the war came, and stayed, and nobody else came along till I brought the head offices here with me. Now I've got a house all to myself.'

'Yeah. Yeah, you're lucky,' said Drummond. He looked out the window, not seeing the sunspattered woods. Presently he asked, his voice a little harsh: 'How is this country doing now? Really doing?'

'For a while it was rough,' said the general. 'Damn rough. When the cities went, our transportation, communication, and distribution systems broke down. In fact, our whole economy fell apart, though not all at once. Then there was the dust and the plagues. People fled, and there was open fighting when over-crowded safe places refused to take in any more refugees. Police went with the cities, and the army couldn't do much patrolling. We were busy fighting the enemy troops that'd flown over the Pole to invade. We still haven't gotten them all. Bands are roaming the country, hungry and desperate outlaws, and there are plenty of Americans who turned to banditry when everything else failed. That's why we have this guard with us, though so far none has come this way.

'The insect and blight weapons just about wiped out our crops, and that winter everybody starved. We checked the pests with modern methods, though it was touch and go for a while, and next year got some food. Of course, with no distribution as yet, we've failed to save a lot of people. And farming is still a tough proposition. We won't really have the bugs licked for a long time. I wish we had a research center as well equipped as those which produced the things. But we're gaining. We're gaining.'

'Distribution –' Drummond rubbed his chin. 'How about railways? Horse-drawn vehicles?'

'We have some railroads going, but the enemy was as careful to hit most of ours as we were to hit theirs. As for horses, there weren't many to start with, and they were nearly all eaten that first winter. I know personally of only a dozen. They're on my place; I'm trying to breed enough to be of use,' Robinson smiled wryly, 'but by the time we've raised that many, the factories should have been going quite a spell.'

'And so now?'

'We're over the worst. Except for outlaws, we have the population fairly well controlled. The civilized people are eating, more or less, and have some kind of housing. We have machine shops, small-town factories, and the like, enough to maintain our economy. Presently we'll be able to expand these, begin actually increasing what we have. In another five years or so, I guess, we'll be integrated enough to drop martial law and hold a general election. A big job ahead, but a good one.'

The car halted to let a cow lumber over the road, a calf trotting at her heels. She was gaunt and shaggy, and skittered nervously into the brush.

'Wild,' explained Robinson. 'Most of the real wild life was killed off for food in the last two years, but a lot of farm animals escaped when their owners died or fled, and have run free ever since.' He noticed Drummond's fixed gaze. The pilot was

13

looking at the calf. Its legs were half the normal length.

'Mutant,' said the general. 'You find a lot of such animals. Radiation from bombed or dusted areas. There are even a lot of abnormal human births.' He scowled, worry clouding his eyes. 'In fact, that's just about our worst problem.'

The car emerged from the woods onto the shore of a small lake. It was a peaceful scene, the quiet waters like molten gold in the slanting sunlight, trees ringing them and the mountains all around. Under one huge pine stood a cottage and a woman on the porch.

It was like one summer with Barbara – Drummond cursed under his breath and followed Robinson toward the little building. It wasn't, it wasn't, it could never be. Not ever again. There were soldiers guarding this place from chance marauders, and an odd-looking flower at his feet, a daisy, but huge and red and irregularly formed.

A squirrel chittered from a tree. Drummond saw that its face was so blunt as to be almost human.

Then he was on the porch, and Robinson was introducing him to 'my wife, Elaine.' She was a nice-looking young woman with eyes that were sympathetic on Drummond's exhausted face. He noticed she was pregnant, and there was a dull marveling in him at the hope which was life.

He was led inside, and reveled in a hot bath. Afterward there was supper, but he was numb with sleep by then, and hardly noticed it when Robinson put him to bed.

2

Reaction set in, and for a week or so Drummond went about in a haze, not much good to himself, or anyone else. But it was surprising what plenty of food and sleep could do, and one evening Robinson came home to find him scribbling on sheets of paper.

'Arranging my notes and so on,' he explained. 'I'll write out the complete report in a month, I guess.'

'Good. But no hurry.' Robinson settled tiredly into an armchair. 'The rest of the world will keep. I'd rather you'd just work at this off and on, and join my staff for your main job.'

'Okay. Only what'll I do?'

'Everything. Specialization is gone: too few surviving specialists and equipment. I think your chief task will be to head the census bureau.'

'Eh?'

Robinson grinned lopsidedly. 'You'll *be* the census bureau, except for what few assistants I can spare you.' He leaned forward and said earnestly, 'And it's one of the most important jobs there is. You'll do for this country what you did for central Eurasia, only in much greater detail. Drummond, we have to *know*.'

He took a map from a desk drawer and spread it out. 'Look, here's the United States. I've marked regions known to be uninhabitable in red.' His fingers traced out the ugly splotches. 'Too many of 'em, and doubtless there are others we haven't found yet. Now, the blue X's are army posts.' They were sparsely scattered over the land, near the centers of population groupings.

'Not enough of those. It's all we can do to control the more or less well-off, orderly people. Bandits, enemy troops, homeless refugees – they're still running wild, skulking in the backwoods and barrens, and raiding whenever they can. And they spread the plague. We won't really have it licked till everybody's settled down, and that'd be hard to enforce. Drummond, we don't even

15

have enough soldiers to start up a feudal system. The plague spread like a prairie fire in those concentrations of men.

'We have to *know*. We have to know how many people survived – half the population, a third, a quarter, whatever it is. We have to know where they go, and how they're fixed for supplies, so we can arrange a fair distribution system. We have to find all the smalltown shops and labs and libraries still standing, and rescue their priceless contents before looters or the weather beat us to it. We have to locate doctors and engineers and other professional men, and put them to work rebuilding. We have to find the outlaws and round them up. We – Hell, I could go on forever. Once we have all that information, we can set up a master plan for redistributing population, agriculture, industry, and the rest most efficiently, for getting the country back under civil authority, for opening regular transportation and communication channels – for getting the nation back on its feet.'

'I see,' nodded Drummond. 'Hitherto, just surviving and hanging on to what was left has taken precedence. Now you're in a position to start expanding, if you know where and how much to expand.'

'Exactly.' Robinson rolled a cigaret, grimacing. 'Not much tobacco left. What I have is pretty foul. Lord, that war was crazy!'

'All wars are,' said Drummond dispassionately, 'but technology advanced to the point of giving us a knife to cut our throats with. Before that, we were just beating our heads against the wall. Robinson, we can't go back to the old ways. We've got to start on a new track – a track of sanity.'

'Yes. And that brings up –' The other man looked toward the kitchen door. They could hear the cheerful rattle of dishes there, and smell mouth-watering cooking odors. Robinson lowered his voice. 'I might as well tell you this now, but don't let Elaine know. She – she shouldn't be worried. Drummond, did you see our horses?'

'The other day, yes. The colts –'

'Uh-huh. There've been five colts born of eleven mares in the last year. Two of them were so deformed they died in a week, another in a few months. One of the two left has cloven hoofs and almost no teeth. The last one looks normal – so far. One out of eleven, Drummond.'

'Were those horses near a radioactive area?'

'Well,' said Robinson, 'the radiation count everywhere is 'way up, of course. If you mean a violently emitting region, though, then they must have been. They were rounded up wherever found and brought here. The stallion was caught near the site of Portland, I know.' Robinson scowled. 'But if he were the only one with mutated genes, it would hardly show in the first generation, would it? I understand nearly all mutations are Mendelian recessives. Even if one were dominant, it ought to show in all the colts – three-fourths of them, I mean – but none of these looked alike.'

'Hmmm – I don't know much about genetics,' said Drummond, 'but I do know hard radiation, or rather the secondary charged particles it produces, can cause mutation. Only mutants are rare, and tend to fall into certain patterns. According to experiments before the war, even a lot of radioactivity isn't supposed to jump the mutation rate of mammals much.'

'So they thought – then!' Suddenly Robinson was grim, and a cold fright lay in his eyes. 'Haven't you noticed the animals and plants? They're fewer than formerly, and . . . well, I've not kept count, but at least half those seen or killed have something wrong, internally or externally.'

Drummond drew heavily on his pipe, needing what small comfort it could give. Very quietly, he said:

'If I remember my college biology right, they told me the vast majority of mutations are unfavorable. More ways of not doing something than of doing it. Radiation might sterilize an animal, or it might produce several degrees of genetic change. You could have a mutation so violently lethal the possessor never gets born, or soon dies. You could have all kinds of more or less handicapping factors, or just random changes not making much difference one way or the other. Or in a few rare cases you might get something actually favorable, but you couldn't really say the possessor is a true member of the species. And favorable mutations themselves usually involve a price in the partial or total loss of some other function.'

'Right.' Robinson nodded bleakly. 'One of your jobs on the census will be to try and locate any and all who know genetics, and send them here. But your real task, which only you and I and a couple of others must know about, the big job, will be to find the human mutants.'

Drummond's throat was dry. 'There've been a lot of them?' he whispered.

'Yes. But we don't know how many or where. We only know about those people who live near an army post, or have some other fairly regular dealings with us, and they're only a few thousand all told. Among them, the birth rate has gone to about half the prewar. And over half the births they do have are abnormal.'

'Over half –'

'Yeah. Of course, the violently different ones soon die, or are put in an institution we've set up in the Alleghenies. But what can we do with the others, if their parents still want them? A kid with deformed or missing or abortive organs, twisted guts, a tail, or something even worse . . . well, *it'll* have a tough time in life, but it can generally survive. And propagate!'

'And a normal-looking one might have some unnoticeable quirk, or a characteristic that won't show up for years. Or even a truly normal one might be carrying recessives, and pass them on – God!' Drummond's exclamation was half blasphemy, half prayer. 'But how'd it happen? People weren't all near atom-bombed or dusted areas.'

'Maybe not,' said Robinson, 'though a lot escaped from the outskirts. But there was that first year, with everybody on the move. You could pass near enough to a blasted region to be affected, without knowing it. And that damned radiodust, blowing on the wind. It's got a long half-life, some of it. It'll be active for decades. Then promiscuity got common, still is, and no contraceptives to be had. Oh, mutations would spread themselves, all right.'

'I still don't see why they spread so much,' said Drummond. 'Even here –'

'Well, I don't know why it shows up here. I suppose the local flora and fauna came in from elsewhere. This place is safe. The nearest dusted area is three hundred miles off, with mountains between. My tame biologist tells me that the radioactivity here, while high enough, isn't sufficient to change mutation rates appreciably – the prewar experiments showed that much. There must be many such islands of comparatively normal conditions. We have to find them too. But elsewhere –'

'Soup's on,' announced Elaine, and went from the kitchen to the dining room with a loaded tray.

The men rose. Drummond looked at Robinson and said tonelessly: 'Okay. I'll get your information for you. We'll map mutation areas and safe areas, we'll check on our population and resources, we'll eventually get all the facts you want. But – what are you going to do then?'

'I wish I knew,' said Robinson. 'I only wish I knew.'

3

Winter lay heavily on the north, a huge gray sky seeming frozen solid over the rolling white plains. The last three winters had come early and stayed long. Colloidal dust of the bombs, suspended in the atmosphere and cutting down the solar constant by a deadly percent or two. There had even been a few earthquakes, set off in geologically unstable parts of the world by bombs planted just right. Half California had been laid waste when a sabotage bomb started the San Andreas Fault on a major slip. And that kicked up still more dust.

Drummond's mind groped back into myth. *Fimbulwinter. The weird of the gods. But no, we're surviving. Though maybe not as men –*

Most people had gone south, and there overcrowding had

made starvation and disease and internecine warfare a normal part of life. Those who'd stuck it out up here, and had some luck with their pest-ridden crops, were better off.

Drummond's jet slid above the cratered black ruin of the Twin Cities. There was still enough radioactivity to melt the snow, and the pit was like a skull's empty eye socket. Drummond sighed, but he was becoming hardened to death. There was so much of it.

He strained through a sinister twilight, swooping low over the unending fields. Burned-out hulks of farmhouses, bones of ghost towns, sere deadness of dusted land – but he'd heard travelers speak of a fairly powerful community up near the Canadian border, and it was up to him to find it.

A lot of things had been up to him in the last six months. He'd had to work out a means of search, and organize his few, over-worked assistants into an efficient staff, and go out on the long hunt.

They hadn't covered the nation. That was impossible. Their few jets had gone to areas chosen more or less at random, trying to get a cross section of conditions. They'd penetrated wilder-nesses of hill and plain and forest, establishing contact with scattered, still demoralized outdwellers. On the whole, it was more laborious than anything else. Most were pathetically glad to see any symbol of law and order and what were already being called the 'old days.'

Now and then there was trouble, when they encountered wary or sullen or openly hostile groups suspicious of a government they associated with disaster, and once there had even been a pitched battle with roving outlaws. But the work had gone ahead, and now the preliminaries were about over.

Preliminaries – It was a bigger job to find out exactly how matters stood than the entire country was capable of undertaking today. But Drummond had enough facts for extrapolation. He and his staff had collected most of the essential data and begun correlating them. By questioning, by observation, by seeking and finding, by any means that came to hand, they'd filled their notebooks. And in the sketchy outlines of a Chinese drawing, and with the same stark reality, the truth was there.

Just this one more place, and I'll go home, thought Drummond for the – thousandth? – time. His brain was getting into a rut, treading the same terrible circle and finding no way out. *Robinson won't like what I tell him, but there it is.* And slowly: *Barbara, maybe it was best you and the kids went as you did. Quickly, cleanly, not even knowing it. This isn't much of a world. It'll never be our world again.*

He saw the place he sought, a huddle of buildings near the frozen shores of the Lake of the Woods, and his jet murmured toward the white ground. The stories he'd heard of this town weren't overly encouraging, but he supposed he'd get out all right. The others had his data anyway, so it didn't matter.

By the time he'd landed in the clearing just outside the village, using the jet's skis, most of the inhabitants were there waiting. In the gathering dusk they were a ragged and wild-looking bunch, clumsily dressed in whatever scraps of cloth and leather they had been able to find. The bearded, hard-eyed men were armed with clubs and knives and a few guns. As Drummond got out, he was careful to keep his hands away from his own automatics.

'Hello,' he said. 'I'm friendly.'

'Y'better be,' growled the big man who seemed their leader. 'Who are you, where from, an' why?'

'First,' lied Drummond smoothly, 'I want to tell you I have another man with a plane who knows where I am. If I'm not back in a certain time, he'll come with bombs. But we don't intend any harm or interference. This is just a sort of social call. I'm Hugh Drummond of the United States Army.'

They digested that slowly. Clearly, they weren't well-disposed toward the government, but they stood in too much awe of aircraft and armament to be openly hostile. The leader spat. 'How long you staying?'

'Just overnight, if you'll put me up. I'll pay for it.' He held up a small pouch. 'Tobacco.'

Their eyes gleamed, and the leader said, 'You'll stay with me. Come on.'

Drummond gave him the bribe and went with the group. He didn't like to spend such priceless luxuries thus freely, but the job was more important. And the boss seemed thawed a little by the fragrant brown flakes. He was sniffing them greedily.

'Been smoking bark an' grass,' he confided. 'Terrible.'

'Worse than that,' agreed Drummond. He turned up his jacket collar and shivered. The wind starting up with dusk was bitterly cold.

'Just what y' here for?' demanded someone else.

'Well, just to see how things stand. We've got the government started again, and are patching things up. But we have to know where the people are, what they need, and so on.'

'Don't want nothin' t' do with the gov'ment,' muttered a woman. 'They brung all this on us.'

'Oh, come now. We didn't ask to be attacked.' Mentally, Drummond crossed his fingers. He neither knew nor cared who was to blame. Both sides, letting mutual fear and friction mount to hysteria – In fact, he wasn't sure the United States hadn't sent out the first rockets, on orders of some panicky or aggressive official. Nobody was alive who admitted knowing.

'It's the jedgment o'God for all our sins,' came a voice out of the thickening twilight. The scrunch of snow under shoes ran beneath the words, as if the earth laughed. 'The plague, the fire-death, the rockets, ain't it foretold in the Bible? Ain't we living in the last days o' the world?'

'Maybe.' Drummond was glad to stop before a long low cabin. Religious argument was touchy at best, and with a lot of people nowadays it was dynamite.

They entered the rudely furnished but fairly comfortable house. A good many crowded in with them. For all their suspicion, they were curious, and an outsider in an aircraft was a blue-moon event.

Drummond's eyes flickered unobtrusively about the room, noticing details. Three women – that meant a return to concubinage; only to be expected in a day of few men and strong-arm rule. Ornaments and utensils, tools and weapons of good quality – yes, that confirmed the stories. This wasn't exactly a bandit town, but it had waylaid travelers and raided other places when times were hard, and built up a sort of dominance of the surrounding country. That too was common.

There was a dog on the floor nursing a litter. Only three pups, and one of those was bald, one lacked ears, and one had more toes than it should. Among the wide-eyed children present, there were several who must have been conceived since the war, and a good fourth of them were visibly monstrous.

Drummond sighed heavily and sat down. In a way, this clinched it. He'd been gathering such evidence for a long time, and finding mutation here, as far as any place from atomic bombing or radiodusting, was about the last proof he needed.

He had to get on friendly terms, or he wouldn't find out much about things like population, food production, and whatever else there was to know. Forcing a smile to stiff lips, he took a flask from his jacket. 'Genuine rye,' he said. 'Who wants a nip?'

'Do we!' The answer barked out in a dozen different voices and words. The flask circulated, men pawing and cursing and grabbing to get it. *Their homebrew must be pretty bad*, thought Drummond wryly.

The chief shouted an order, and one of his women got busy at the primitive stove. 'Rustle you a mess o' chow,' he said with a measure of geniality. 'An' my name's Sam Buckman.'

'Glad to know you, Sam.' Drummond squeezed the hairy paw hard. He had to show he wasn't a weakling, a conniving city slicker.

'What's it like, outside?' asked someone presently. 'We ain't heard for so long.'

'You haven't missed much,' said Drummond, attacking the food that was set before him. It was pretty good, considering. Briefly, he sketched conditions. 'You're better off than most,' he finished.

'Yeah. Mebbe so.' Sam Buckman scratched his tangled beard. 'What I'd give f'r a razor blade! It ain't easy, though. The first year we weren't better off'n anyone else. Me, I'm a farmer. I kept some ears o' corn an' a little wheat an' barley in my pockets all that winter, even though I was starving. A bunch o' hungry refugees plundered my place, but I got away an' drifted up here. Next year I took over an empty farm hereabouts an' started over.'

Drummond doubted that it had been abandoned, but said nothing. Sheer survival outweighed law.

'Others came an' settled here,' said the leader reminiscently. 'We farm together. We have to; one man couldn't live by hisself,

23

not with the bugs an' the blight, an' the crops sprouting into all new kinds, an' the outlaws around. Not many up here, though we did beat off some enemy troops last winter.' He glowed with pride at that, but Drummond wasn't particularly impressed. A handful of freezing starveling conscripts, lost and bewildered in a hostile foreign land, with no hope of ever getting home, weren't formidable.

'Things getting better, though,' said Buckman. 'We're heading up.' He scowled, and a palpable chill crept through the room. 'If 'tweren't for the births.'

'Yes – the births. The new babies. Even the stock an' plants.' It was an old man speaking, his eyes glazed with something near to madness. 'It's the mark o' the beast. Satan is loose in the world.'

'Shut up!' Huge and bristling, Buckman launched himself out of his seat and grabbed the oldster by his scrawny throat. 'Shut up 'r I'll bash your lying head in. Ain't no son o' mine being marked by the devil!'

'Or mine –' 'Or mine –' The rumble of voices ran about the cabin, sullen and afraid.

'It's God's jedgment, I tell you!' The woman was shrilling again. 'The end o' the world is near. Prepare for the second coming.'

'An' you shut up too, Mag Schmidt,' snarled Buckman. He stood bent over her, gnarled arms swinging loose, little eyes darting red and wild about the room. 'Shut y'r trap an' keep it shut. I'm still boss here, an' if you don't like it you can get out. I still don't think that funny-looking brat o' y'rs fell in the lake by accident.'

The woman shrank back, her lips tight. The room filled with a crackling silence through which Drummond could hear the jeering of the wind. One of the babies began to cry. It had two heads.

Slowly and heavily, Buckman turned to Drummond, who sat immobile against the wall. 'You see?' he asked dully. 'You see how it is? Maybe it is the curse o' God, I dunno. Maybe the world is ending. I just know there's few enough babies, an' most o' them *de*formed. Will it go on? Will all our kids be monsters? Should we . . . kill these an' hope we get some human babies? What is it? What to do?'

Drummond rose. He felt a weight as of centuries on his shoulders, the weariness, blank and absolute, of having seen that smoldering panic and heard that desperate appeal too often, too often.

'Don't kill them,' he said. 'That's the worst kind of murder, and anyway it'd do no good at all. It comes from the bombs, and you can't stop it. You'll go right on having such children, so you might as well get used to it.'

4

By atomic-powered stratojet it wasn't far from Minnesota to Oregon, and Drummond landed in Taylor about noon the next day. This time there was no hurry to get his machine under cover, and up on the mountain was a raw scar of earth where a new airfield was slowly being built. Men were getting over their terror of the sky. They had another fear to live with now, and it was one from which there was no hiding.

Drummond walked down the icy main street to the central office. It was numbingly cold, a still, relentless intensity of frost eating through clothes and flesh and bone. It wasn't much better inside. The fuel shortage made heating systems a joke.

'You're back!' Robinson met him in the antechamber, suddenly galvanized with eagerness. He had grown thin and nervous, he looked ten years older, but impatience blazed from him. 'How is it? How is it?'

Drummond held up a bulky notebook. 'All here,' he said tonelessly. 'All the facts we'll need. Not formally correlated yet, but the picture is simple enough.'

Robinson took his arm and steered him into the office. He felt

25

the general's hand shaking, but he'd sat down and had a drink before business came up again.

'You've done a good job,' said the leader warmly. 'When the country's organized again, I'll see you get a medal for this. Your men in the other planes aren't in yet.'

'No, they'll be surveying for a long time. The job won't be finished for years. I've only got a sort of outline here, but it's enough. It's enough.' Drummond's eyes were haunted.

Robinson felt cold at meeting that too-steady gaze. He whispered shakily: 'Is it – bad?'

'The worst. Physically, the country's recovering. But biologically, we've reached a crossroads and taken the wrong fork.'

'What do you mean? *What do you mean?*'

Drummond let him have it then, straight and hard as a bayonet thrust. 'The birth rate's a little over half the prewar,' he said, 'and about seventy-five percent of all births are mutant, of which possibly two-thirds are viable and presumably fertile. Of course, that doesn't include late-maturing characteristics, or those undetectable by naked-eye observation, or the mutated recessive genes that must be carried by all of us. And it's everywhere. There are no safe places.'

'I see,' said Robinson after a long time. He nodded, like a man struck a stunning blow and not yet fully aware of it. 'The reason –'

'Is obvious.'

'Yes. People going through radioactive areas –'

'Why, no. That would only account for a few, if any at all. Remember those old experimental results. Temporary irradiation just doesn't produce mutation on that scale.'

'No matter. The fact's there, and that's enough. We have to decide what to do about it.'

'And soon.' Drummond's jaw tightened. 'It's wrecking our civilization. We at least preserved our cultural continuity, but even that's going now. People are going crazy as birth after birth is monstrous. Fear of the unknown, striking at minds still sick from the war and its aftermath. Frustration of parenthood, perhaps the most basic instinct there is. It's leading to infanticide, desertion, despair, a cancer at the root of society. We've got to act.'

'How? How?' Robinson stared down at his hands.

'I don't know. You're the leader. Maybe an educational campaign, though that doesn't sound too practicable. Maybe an acceleration of your program for re-integrating the country. Maybe – I don't know.'

Drummond stuffed tobacco into his pipe. He was near the end of his supply, but would rather take a few good smokes than a lot of niggling puffs. 'Of course,' he said thoughtfully, 'it's probably not the end of things. We won't know for a generation or more, but I rather imagine the mutants can grow into society. They'd better, for they'll outnumber the humans. The thing is, if we just let matters drift there's no telling where they'll go. The situation is unprecedented. We may end up as a culture of specialized variations, which would be very bad from an evolutionary standpoint. There may be fighting between mutant types, or with humans. Interbreeding may produce worse freaks, particularly when accumulated recessives start showing up. Robinson, if we want any say at all in what's going to happen in the next few centuries, we have to act quickly. Otherwise it'll snowball out of all control.'

'Yes. Yes, we'll have to act fast. And hard.' Robinson straightened in his chair. Decision firmed his countenance, but his eyes were staring. 'We're mobilized,' he said. 'We have the men and weapons and the organization. They won't be able to resist.'

Drummond felt a swift and horrible wrenching of fear. 'What are you getting at?' he snapped.

'Racial death. All mutants and their parents to be sterilized whenever and wherever detected.'

'You're crazy!' Drummond sprang from his seat, grabbed Robinson's shoulders across the desk, and shook him. 'You . . . why, it's impossible! You'll bring revolt, civil war, final collapse!'

'Not if we go about it right.' Sweat studded the general's forehead. 'I don't like it any better than you, but it's got to be done or the human race is finished. Normal births are rare.' He surged to his feet, gasping. 'I've thought a long time about this. I've studied the thing. Your facts only confirmed my suspicions.

This tears it. Can't you see? Evolution has to proceed slowly. Life wasn't meant for such a storm of change. Unless we can save the true human stock, it'll be absorbed, and the changes will go on and on and on. Or there must be a lot of lethal recessives.

'In a large population, they can accumulate unnoticed till nearly everybody has them, and then start emerging all at once. That would nearly wipe us out. It's happened before, population cycles in rats and lemmings and – If we eliminate mutant stock now, we can still save the race. It won't be cruel. We can sterilize so it won't make any difference, except that those people won't have children. But it's got to be done.' His voice broke on a scream. 'It's got to be done!'

Drummond slapped him, hard. Robinson drew a shuddering breath, sat down, and began to cry, and somehow that was the most horrible sight of all.

'You're crazy,' said Drummond. 'You've gone nuts with brooding alone on this the last six months, without knowing or being able to act. You've lost all perspective.'

After a moment, he continued: 'We can't use violence. In the first place, it would break our cracked and shaking civilization for good, into a mad-dog finish fight. We'd not even win. We're outnumbered, and we couldn't hold down a continent, eventually a planet. And remember what we said once, about leaving the old savage way of settling things, that never brings a settlement at all? We'd throw away a lesson our noses were rubbed in not three years ago. We'd commit race suicide just because we were scared to go on living.'

Robinson didn't reply, and Drummond went on very quietly: 'And anyway, it wouldn't do a bit of good. Mutants would still be born. The poison is everywhere. Normal parents will still give birth to mutants, somewhere along the line. We just have to accept that fact, and adjust to it. The *new* human race will have to.'

'I'm sorry.' Robinson raised a ghastly face from his hands, but there was a certain calm on it now. 'I . . . blew my top. You're right. I've been thinking of this, worrying and wondering, lying awake nights, and when I finally sleep I dream of it. I – Yes, I see your point. And you're right.'

'It's okay. You've been under a terrific strain. Three years with never a rest, and the responsibility for a nation, and now this. Sure, everybody's entitled to be a little crazy. We'll work out a solution, somehow.'

'Yes, of course.' Robinson poured out two stiff drinks and gulped his own. He paced restlessly, with a rising strength. 'Let me see – Eugenics, of course. If we work hard, we'll have the nation tightly organized inside of ten years. Then . . . well, I don't suppose we can keep the mutants from interbreeding, but certainly we can pass laws to protect humans and encourage their propagation. Since radical mutations would probably be inter-sterile anyway, and most mutants handicapped one way or another, a few generations should see humans completely dominant again.'

Drummond frowned. He was worried. It wasn't like Robinson to be so unreasonable. Somehow, the man had acquired a blind spot where this most ultimate of human problems was concerned. He said slowly: 'That won't work either. First, it'd be hard to impose and enforce. Second, we'd be repeating the old *Herrenvolk* fallacy. Mutants are inferior, mutants must be kept in their place – to enforce that, especially on a majority, you'd need a full-fledged totalitarian state. Third, that wouldn't work either, for the rest of the world, with almost no exceptions, is under no such control. And we won't be in a position to rule them for a long time – generations, probably. Before then, mutants will dominate everywhere over there, and if they resent the way we treat their kind here, we'd better run for cover.'

'You assume a lot. How do you know those hundreds or thousands of different types will work together? They're less like each other than like us, even. They could be played off against each other.'

'Maybe. But *that* would be going back onto the old road of treachery and violence, the road to Hell. Conversely, if every not-quite-human is called a 'mutant', like a separate class, he'll think he is, and act accordingly against the lumped-together 'humans.' No, the only way to sanity – to survival – is to abandon class prejudice and race hate altogether, and work as individuals. We're all – well, Earthlings – and subclassification is deadly. We all have to live together, and might as well make the best of it.' Drummond smiled with little mirth. 'End of sermon.'

'Yeah . . . yeah, I guess you're right, at that.'

'Anyway,' said Drummond, 'I repeat that all such attempts would be useless. All Earth is infected with mutation. It will be for a long time. The purest human stock will still produce freaks.'

'Y-yes, that's true. Our best bet seems to be to find all such stock and withdraw it into the few safe areas left. It'll mean a small human population, but a *human* one.'

'I tell you, that's impossible!' snapped Drummond. 'There are no safe places. Not one.'

Robinson stopped pacing and looked at Drummond as at a physical antagonist. 'That so?' he almost growled. 'Why?'

Drummond told him, adding incredulously. 'Surely you knew that. Your physicists have measured the amount of it. Your doctors, your engineers, that geneticist I dug up for you. You obviously got a lot of those biological technicalities you've been slinging at me from him. They must all have told you the same thing!'

Robinson shook his head stubbornly. 'It can't be. It's not reasonable. The concentration wouldn't be great enough.'

'Why, you poor fool, you need only look around you. The plants, the animals! Haven't there been any human births here?'

'No. This is still a man's town, though women are trickling in and several babies are on the way.' Robinson's face twisted. 'Elaine's is due any time now. She's in the hospital. Don't you see, our other kids died of the plague. This one's all we have. We want him to grow up in the right kind of world – not the one we've got now. You and I are on our way out. We're the old gene-ration, the one that wrecked the world. It's up to us to build it again, and then back out and let our children have it. But we've got to make it ready for them, don't we? Don't we?'

Sudden insight held Drummond motionless for long seconds. Understanding came, and pity, and an odd gentleness that changed his sunken bony face. 'Yes,' he murmured, 'yes, I see. That's why you're working with all that's in you to build a healthy future. That's why you nearly went crazy when this

30

threat appeared. That ... that's why you just can't comprehend.'

He put his arm around the other man's shoulder and guided him toward the door. 'Come on,' he said. 'Let's go see how your wife's making out. Maybe we can get some flowers on the way.'

5

The silent cold bit at them as they went down the street. Snow crackled underfoot. It was already grimy with town smoke and dust, but overhead the sky was incredibly clean and blue. Breath smoked whitely from their mouths and nostrils. The sound of men at work rebuilding drifted faintly between the bulking mountains.

'We couldn't emigrate to another planet, could we?' asked Robinson, and answered himself: 'No, we lack the organization and resources. They aren't habitable anyway. We'll have to make out on Earth. A few safe spots – there *must* be others besides this one – to house the true humans till the mutation period is over. Yes, we can do it.'

'There are no safe places,' insisted Drummond. To change the subject: 'How does your geneticist think this'll come out, biologically speaking?'

'He doesn't know. His specialty is still largely unknown. He can make an intelligent guess, and that's all.'

'Yeah. Anyway, our problem is to learn to live with the mutants, to accept anyone as – Earthling – no matter how he looks, to quit thinking anything was ever settled by violence. Funny,' mused Drummond, 'how the impractical virtues have become the basic necessities of survival. Maybe it was always true, but it took a beating like this one to make us see that simple fact. Now we've got to convince the rest of the world. I wonder if we can.'

They found some flowers, potted in a house, and Robinson bought them with the last of his tobacco. By the time he reached the hospital, he was sweating. The sweat froze on his face as he walked.

The medical center was the town's largest building, and fairly well-equipped. A nurse met them as they entered.

'I was just going to send for you, General Robinson,' she said. 'The baby's on the way.'

'How . . . is she?'

'Fine, so far. Just wait here, please.'

'Drummond sank into a chair and watched Robinson's jerky pacing. *The poor guy. The poor damned guy. Why is it expectant fathers are supposed to be so funny? It's like laughing at a man on the rack. I know, Barbara. I know.*

'They have some anesthetics, at least,' muttered the general. 'They – Elaine never was very strong.'

'She'll be all right.' *It's afterward that worries me.*

'Yeah – Yeah – How long, though? How long does it take?'

'Depends. Take it easy.' With a wrench, Drummond made a sacrifice to a man he liked. He filled his pipe and handed it over. 'Here, you need a smoke.'

'Thanks.' Robinson puffed raggedly.

The slow minutes passed, fading into hours, and Drummond wondered vaguely what he would do when – *it* – happened. It didn't have to happen. But the chances were all against such an easy solution. He was no psychiatrist. Best to let things occur as they would.

The waiting broke at last. A doctor came out, inscrutable in his robe. Robinson stood before him, motionless.

'You're a brave man,' said the doctor. His face was bleak as he took off the mask. 'You'll need your courage.'

'She –' It was hardly a human sound.

'Your wife is doing well. But the baby –'

A nurse brought out the little wailing form. It was a boy. But his limbs were limp rubbery tentacles.

Robinson looked, and something went out of him as he stood

there. When he turned, he wore a dead man's face.

'You're lucky,' said Drummond, and meant it. He'd seen too many other mutants. 'After all, he can learn to use those – arms. Maybe surgery can help. He'll get along all right. He might even have an advantage for certain types of work. It isn't a deformity, really. If there's nothing else, you've got a good kid.'

'*If!*' whispered Robinson. 'How can you tell?'

'You can't yet. But you've got guts, you and Elaine. You'll make out, together.' *Yes, together*, thought Drummond, and went on swiftly:

'I see why you didn't understand the problem. You *wouldn't*. It was a psychological block, suppressing a fact you didn't dare face. That boy was the big hope of your life. You couldn't think the truth about him and his chances, so your subconscious just refused to let you think rationally on the subject of mutation at all.

'Now you know. Now you realize there is no hiding place, not anywhere in the world. The tremendous incidence of mutant births in the first generation should have told you that by itself. Most such new traits are recessive, which means both parents have to have it for it to show in the child. But genetic changes are random, except for a tendency to fall into roughly similar patterns – four-leaved clovers or albinos, for instance. Think how big the total number of such changes must be, to produce so many corresponding alterations in male *and* female these past three years. Think how many, *many* recessives there must be, existing only in gene patterns till their mates show up. We'll just have to take our chances on something deadly accumulating. We'd never know till too late.'

'The dust –' faltered Robinson.

'Yeah. The radiodust. Its colloidal, and uncountable other radio-colloids were formed when the bombs went off, and ordinary dirt and air gets into unstable isotopic forms near the craters. The poison is all over the world by now, blown on the wind.

'The concentration isn't too high for life, though it's pretty near the safe limit and there'll probably be a lot of cancer. But it's everywhere. Every breath we draw, every crumb we eat and drop we drink, every clod we walk on, the radiation is there. It's up in the stratosphere and down under the ground. And there's no escape, for its damage has already been done to us.

'Mutations were rare before, because a charged particle has to get pretty close to a gene and be moving fast before its electromagnetic effects cause chemical change, and then that particular chromosome has to enter into reproduction. But now the charged particles, and the gamma rays producing still more, are everywhere. Many genes themselves must contain radioactive atoms.

'Even at the comparatively low concentration, the odds favor a given organism having so many cells changed that at least one will give rise to a mutant when it reproduces. There's even a good chance of like recessives meeting in the first generation, as we've seen. Nobody is safe, no place is free.'

'The geneticist,' said Robinson mechanically, 'thinks some true humans will continue.'

'A few, probably. After all, the radioactivity isn't too concentrated, and it's burning itself out. But it'll take fifty or a hundred years for it to drop to insignificance, and by then the "pure" stock will be 'way in the minority. And there'll still be all those unmatched recessives, waiting to show up.'

'You were right. We should never have created science. It brought the end of the race.'

'I didn't say that. The race brought its own destruction, through misuse of science. Our culture was scientific anyway, in all except its psychological basis. It's up to us to take that last and hardest step. If we do, man – or man's descendants – may yet survive.'

Drummond gave Robinson a gentle push toward the inner door. 'You're exhausted, beat up, ready to quit,' he said. 'It'll look different tomorrow. Go on in and see Elaine. Give her my regards. Then take a long rest before going back to work. I still think you've got a good kid.'

Mechanically, the *de facto* President of the United States left the room. Hugh Drummond stared after him a moment, then went out into the street, zipping up his jacket against the cold.

Chain of Logic

Brother bringeth
brother his bane,
and sons of sisters
split kinship's bonds.
Not ever a man
spareth another.
Hard is the world.
Whoredom waxeth.
Ax-time, sword-time,
– shields are cloven –
wind-time and wolf-time,
ere the world waneth.
*   – Elder Edda*

1

He was nearly always alone, and even when others were beside him, even when he was speaking with them, he seemed to be standing on the far side of an unbridgeable gulf. His only companion was a gaunt gray mongrel with a curiously shaped head and savage disposition, and the two had traveled far over the empty countryside, the rolling plains and straggling woods and high bluffs that went for miles down the river. They were an uncanny sight, walking along a ridge against the blood-flaring sunset, the thin, ragged, big-headed boy like a dwarf from some legend and the shaggy, lumpish animal skulking at his heels.

Roderick Wayne saw them thus as he walked home along the river. They were trotting rapidly on the other side. He hailed them, and they stopped, and the boy stared curiously, almost wonderingly. Wayne knew that attitude, though Alaric was only a gargoyle outline against the fantastically red sky. He knew that his son was looking and looking at him, as if trying to focus, as if trying to remember who the – stranger – was. And the old pain lay deep in him, though he called loudly enough: 'Come on over, Al!'

Wayne had had a hard day's work in the shop, and he was tired. Fixing machines was a long jump down from teaching mathematics in Southvale College, but the whole world had fallen and men survived as best they could in its ruins. He was better off than most – couldn't complain.

Of old he had been wont to stroll by the river that traversed the campus, each evening after classes, smoking his pipe and swinging his cane, thinking perhaps of what Karen would have for supper or of the stark impersonal beauty of the latest development in quantum mechanics – two topics not as unrelated as one might suppose. The quiet summer dusks were not to be spent in worry or petty plans for the next day, there was always time enough for that. He simply walked along in his loose-jointed fashion, breathing tobacco smoke and the cool still air, watching the tall old trees mirror themselves in the water of the molten gold and copper of sunset. There would be a few students on the broad smooth lawns, who would hail him in a friendly way, for Bugsy Wayne was well liked – otherwise only the river and himself and the evening star.

But that was sixteen or more years ago, and his memories of it were dim by now. The brief, incredible nightmare of a war that wiped out every important city in the world in a couple of months – its long-drawn aftermath of diseases, starvation, battle, work, woe, and the twisting of human destiny – that covered those earlier days, distorting them like rocks seen through a flowing stream. Now the campus stood in ruinous desolation, cattle staked out in the long grass, crumbling empty buildings staring with blind eyes at the shards of man.

After the cities went and the world's culture shattered into a fratricidal fighting for scraps, there was no more need for professors but a desperate shortage of mechanics and technicians. Southvale, a sleepy college town in the agricultural Midwest, drew itself into a tight communistic dictatorship to defend what it had. Those had been cruel times, when every stranger was met with guns. There had been open battles with wandering starvelings.

But the plagues were kept out, and they had saved enough food for most of them to survive even that first winter. Thereafter, farm machinery had to be kept going. When the gasoline gave out, it had to be converted to the power of horse, mule, ox, and man. So Wayne had been assigned to the machine shop and, somewhat to his own surprise, turned out to be an excellent technician. His talent for robbing now useless tractors and automobiles in search of spare parts for the literally priceless food machines got his nickname changed to Cannibal, and he rose to general superintendent.

That was a long time ago, and things had improved since. The dictatorship was gone now, and Southvale was again a part of the nation. But it still didn't need professors, and it had enough elementary teachers for its waning child population. So Wayne was still machine-shop boss. In spite of which, he was only a very tired man in patched and greasy overalls, going home to supper, and his thoughts darkened as he saw his child.

Alaric Wayne crossed the bridge a few yards upriver and joined his father. They were an odd contrast; the man tall and stooped, with grayed hair and a long, lined face; the boy small for his fourteen years, lean and ragged, his frail-looking body a little too short for his long legs, his head a little too big for both. Under ruffled brown hair his face was thin, straight-lined and delicately cut, but the huge light-blue eyes were vacant.

'Where've you been all day, son?' asked Wayne. He didn't really expect an answer, and got none. Alaric rarely spoke, didn't even seem to hear most questions. He was looking ahead now like a blind creature, but for all his gawky appearance there was a certain grace in his movements.

Wayne's glance held only pity, and there was an infinite weariness in his mind. *This is the future. This was man's decision, to sell his birthright, his racial existence, for the sovereign prerogatives of nations existing today only in name and memory. And what will come of it, no one can know.*

They walked up a hill and onto the street. Grass had grown between paving blocks, and tumble-down houses stood empty in weed-covered lots. A little farther on, they came into the district still inhabited. The population had fallen to about half the prewar, through privation and battle and sterility, and there had been little immigration since the restrictions were lifted.

At first glance, Southvale had a human, almost medieval look. A horse-drawn wagon creaked by. Folk went down toward the market place in rude homespun clothes, carrying torches and clumsy lanterns. Candlelight shone warmly through the windows of tenanted houses.

Then you saw the dogs and horses and cattle more closely – and the children.

A pack of grimy urchins went by, normal by the old standards, normal too in their shouting spite: 'Mutie! Mutie! Yaaah, mu-*tunt!*' Alaric did not seem to notice them, but his dog bristled and growled. In the dusk the animal's high round head, hardly canine, seemed demoniac, and his eyes gleamed red.

Another band of children went by, as dirty and tattered as the first, but – not human. Mutant. No two alike. A muzzled beast face. A finger less or a finger more than five. Feet like toeless, horny-skinned hoofs, twisted backs, grotesque limping gait. Pattering dwarfs. Acromegalic giants, seven feet tall at six years of age. A bearded six-year-old. And worse.

Not all were obviously deformed. Most mutations were, naturally, unfavorable, but none in that group was cripplingly handicapped. Several looked entirely normal, and their internal differences had been discovered more or less accidentally. Probably many of the 'human' children had some such variation, unsuspected, or a latent mutation that would show up later. Nor were all the deviations deformities. Extremely long legs, or an abnormally high metabolism, for instance, had advantages as well as drawbacks.

Those were the two kinds of children in Southvale and, by report, the world. A third pitiful group hardly counted, that of hopelessly crippled mutants, born with some handicap of mind or body which usually killed them in a few years.

Wayne remembered the horror and despair following the postwar tide of abnormal births, the abortion and infanticide and pogroms. It had faded, of necessity. People knew their child had about three chances in four of being mutant to a greater or lesser degree – but after all, there *could* be a human, if not this time then next, and asylums were maintained for the unwanted young. There could even be a genuinely favorable mutation.

But Wayne had not seen or heard of any such, and in spite of all the wild superman stories doubted that he ever would. There were so many ways of not doing something, so few ways of shaping life right. Even unquestionably good characteristics were, through chance, usually accompanied by a loss elsewhere – like the Martin kid, with his eagle-keen eyes and total deafness.

Wayne waved to that boy, running along with the mutie band, and got an answer. The rest ignored him. Mutants were shy of humans, often resentful and suspicious. And one could hardly blame them. This first generation had been hounded unmercifully by the normal children as it grew up, and had had to endure a lot of abuse and discrimination on the part of adults. Today, with most of their persecutors mature, the mutants were a majority among the children, but they still had little to do with humans of their generation beyond a few fights. The older ones generally realized that *they* would inherit the earth, and were content to wait. Old age and death were their allies.

But Alaric – the ancient uncertain pain stirred in Wayne. He didn't know. Certainly the boy was mutant; an X-ray, taken when the town's machine had recently been put back into service, had shown his internal organs to be reversed in position. That meant little, it had happened before the war now and then, but apparently he also had moronic traits; for he spoke so little and so poorly, had flunked out of elementary school, and seemed wholly remote from the world outside him. But – well, the kid read omnivorously, and at tremendous speed if he wasn't just idly turning pages. He tinkered with apparatus Wayne had salvaged from the abandoned college labs, though there seemed to be no particular purpose in his actions. And every now and then he made some remark which might be queerly significant – unless, of course, that was only his parents' wishful thinking.

Well, Alaric was all they had now. Little Ike, born before the war, had died of hunger the first winter. Since Al's birth they'd had no more children. The radioactivity seemed to have a slow sterilizing effect on many people. And Al was a good kid – well-behaved, shy but not without affection; perhaps all you could really say against him was that he lacked color.

They reached their own home, and Karen met them at the door. The mere sight of her blonde vivacity was enough to lift Wayne's spirits. 'Hello, gentlemen,' she said. 'Guess what?'

'I wouldn't know,' answered Wayne.

'Government jet was here today. We're going to get regular air service.'

'No kidding!'

'Honest Injun. I have it straight from the pilot, a colonel no less. I was down by the field, on the way to market, about noon, when it landed, and of course forced my way into the conversation.'

'You wouldn't have to,' said Wayne admiringly.

'Flatterer! Anyway, he was informing the mayor officially, and a few passers-by like myself threw in their two bucks' worth.'

'Hmmm.' Wayne entered the house. 'Of course, I knew the government was starting an airline, but I never thought we'd get a place on it, even if we do have a cleared space euphemistically termed an airport.'

'Anyway, think of it. Think of the business that'll be coming in. And we'll be getting clothes, fuel, machinery, food – no, I suppose we'll be shipping that ourselves. Apropos which, soup's a-boiling.'

It was a good meal, plain ingredients but imaginative preparation. Wayne attacked it vigorously, but his mind was restless. 'Funny,' he mused, 'how our civilization overreached itself. It grew topheavy and collapsed in a war so great we had to start almost from scratch again. But we had some machines, and enough knowledge to rebuild without too many intervening steps. Our railroads and highways, for instance, are gone, but now we're replacing them with a national airline. Likewise, I imagine later we'll go direct from foot and horseback to private planes.'

'And we won't be isolated any more,' said Karen eagerly. 'We won't be contacting the outside world maybe four times a year. We'll be part of the world again.'

'Mmmm – what's left of it, and that isn't much. Europe and most of Asia, I'm told, are too far gone to count; the southern parts of this country are still pretty savage.'

'It'll be a curious new culture,' said Karen thoughtfully. 'Scattered towns and villages, connected by airlines so fast that cities probably won't need to grow up again. Stretches of wild country in between, and – well, it'll be strange.'

'Certainly that,' said Wayne. 'But we can hardly extrapolate at this stage of the game. Look, in places like this one people are pretty well back on their feet – blights and bugs and plagues just about licked, outlaws rounded up or gone into remote areas. Martial law was – ah – undeclared nine years ago, when the U.S. and Canada were formally united and Hugh Drummond was elected President.'

'I know a little of that already, O omniscient one. What are you leading up to?'

'Simply this. In spite of all which has been accomplished, there's still a long way to go. South of us is anarchic barbarism.

We have precarious contact with some towns and districts in Latin America, Russia, China, Australia, South Africa, and a few other areas. But apart from that we – northern North America – are an island of civilization in a planetary sea of savagery. What will come of that? I can't predict it. Or still more important – what will come of the mutants?'

Karen's eyes were suddenly haggard as they searched Alaric's unheeding face. 'Perhaps at last–the superman,' she whispered.

'Not at all probable, dear, even if that has been the great legend of the postwar world. You know how many mutated recessive genes there must still be, to show up unpredictably in all the centuries to come. There can be no family line on Earth which won't produce sports sometime in the next few generations. And so few of those characteristics can be favorable. God only knows what the end result will be – but it won't be human.'

'There may be other senses of that word.'

'There will be. But they won't be today's.'

'Still,' said Karen wistfully, 'if all the favorable changes showed up in one individual, wouldn't he be a superman?'

'You assume no unfavorable ones, possibly linked, will appear. And the odds against it are unguessable. Anyway, what is a superman? Is he a bulletproof organism of a thousand horsepower? Is he a macrocephalic dwarf talking in symbolic logic formulas? I suppose you mean a godlike being, a greatly refined and improved human. I grant you, a few minor changes in human physique would be desirable, though not at all necessary. But any psychologist will tell you Homo sapiens is a long way from realizing the full capacities he's already got. He needs training right now, not evolution.

'In any case,' finished Wayne flatly, 'we're arguing a dead issue. Homo sapiens has committed race suicide. The mutants will *be* man.'

'Yes – I suppose so. What do you think of the steak?'

After supper, Wayne settled down in his easy chair. Tobacco and newspapers were still unavailable, and the government was still taking all the radios and teevees produced in its new or revived factories. But he had a vast library, his own books and those he had rescued from the college, and most of them were timeless. He opened a well-thumbed little volume and glanced at lines he knew by heart.

> *'For a' that an' a' that,*
> *It's comin' yet for a' that,*
> *When men to men, the whole world o'er,*
> *Shall brothers be for a' that.'*

I wonder. How often I've wondered! And even if Burns was right, will the plowman's common sense apply to non-humanness? Let's see what another old drunkard has to say –

> *'And we, that now make merry in the Room*
> *They left, and Summer dresses in new bloom,*
> *Ourselves must we beneath the Couch of Earth*
> *Descend – ourselves to make a Couch – for whom?'*

His gaze went to Alaric. The boy sprawled on the floor in a litter of open books. His eyes darted from one to another, skipping crazily, their blankness become a weird blue flicker. The books – *Theory of Functions, Nuclear Mechanics, Handbook of Chemistry and Physics, Principles of Psychology, Thermodynamics, Rocket Engineering, Introduction to Biochemistry* – None of it could be skimmed through, or alternated that way. The greatest genius in all history couldn't have done it. And a senseless jumble like that . . . no, Alaric was just turning pages. He must be only a – moron?

Well, I'm tired. Might as well go to bed. Tomorrow's Sunday – good thing we can take holidays again, and sleep late.

2

There were some fifty men in Richard Hammer's gang, and about ten women equally gaunt and furtive and dangerous. They moved slowly along the riverbank, cursing the rocks they stumbled on, but in a ferocious whisper. Overhead a half moon gave vague light from a cloudy sky. The river sped on its way, moonlight shimmering fitfully off its darkness, and an uncertain wind ghosted through soughing trees. Somewhere a dog howled, and a wild cow bellowed alarm for her calf. The night was cool and damp and waiting.

'Dick! How much longer, Dick?'

Hammer turned at the low call and scowled back at the dim forms of his followers. 'Shut up,' he growled. 'No talkin' on march.'

'I'll talk when I please.' The voice was louder.

Hammer hunched his great shoulders and thrust his battered hairy face aggressively into the moonlight. 'I'm still boss,' he said quietly. 'Anytime you want to fight me for the job, go ahead.'

He had their only remaining firearm, a rifle slung over his back and a belt with a few cartridges, but with knife and club, fists and feet and teeth, he was also their hardest battler. That was all which had kept him alive, those unending years of feud and famine and hopeless drifting, for no gangman was ever safe and a boss, with his own jealous underlings to watch as well as outsiders, least of all.

'Okay, okay,' yielded the other man sullenly. 'Only I'm tired an' hungry, we been goin' so long.'

'Not much further,' promised Hammer. 'I rec'nize this territory. Come on – an' quiet!'

They moved ahead, groping, half asleep with weariness, and the gnawing in their bellies was all that kept them going. It had been a long journey, hundreds of miles of devastated southland, and it was bitterly hard to pass these rich northern farms on a night march without lifting more than a few chickens or ears of corn. But Hammer was insistent on secrecy, and he had dominated them long enough for most of them to give in without argument. He had not yet chosen to reveal his full plan, but this far into civilized country it must involve fighting. And looting, the wolf-thought added.

The moon was low when Hammer called a halt. They had topped a high ridge overlooking a darker mass some two miles off, a town. 'Y'all can sleep now,' said the chief. 'We'll hit 'em shortly before sunrise. We'll take the place – food, houses, women, likker! An' more'n that, boys.'

The gang was too tired to care about anything but sleep. They stretched on the ground, lank animal figures in clumsy rags of leather and homespun, carrying knives and clubs, scythes, axes, even spears and bows. Hammer squatted motionless, a great bearded gorilla of a man, his massive face turned toward the sleeping town. A pair of his lieutenants, lean young men with something of ultimate hardness about them, joined him.

'Okay, Dick, what's the idea?' muttered one. 'We don't just go tearin' in; if that was all, there're towns closer to where we come from. What're you cookin' now?'

'Plenty,' said Hammer. 'Now don't get noisy, an' I'll explain. My notion'll give us more'n a few days' food an' rest an' celebration. It'll give us – home.'

'Home!' whispered the other outlaw. His cold eyes took on an odd remote look. 'Home! The word tastes queer. I ain't spoke it so long –'

'I useta live here, before the war,' said Hammer, softly and tonelessly. 'When things blew up, though, I was in the army. The plagues hit my unit, an' them as didn't die the first week went over the hill. I headed south, figgerin' the country'd busted up an' I'd better go where it'd be warm. Only too many other people got the same idea.'

'You've tol' us that much before.'

'I know, I know, but – anybody who lived through it can't forget it. I still see those men dyin' – the plague eatin' 'em. Well, we fought for food. Sep'rate gangs attacked each other when they met. Until at last there was few enough left an' things picked up a little. So I j'ined a village an' started farmin'.'

The dog howled again, closer. There was an eerie quavering in that cry, something never voiced before the mutations began. 'That goddam mutt'll wake the whole muckin' town,' grumbled one of the gangmen.

'Nah, this place been peaceful too long,' said Hammer. 'You can see that. No guards nowhere. Why, there're sep'rate farms. *We* had to fight other men, an' then when we finally planted, there was the bugs an' the blights, an' at last the floods washed our land from under us an' I had to take to gang life again. Then I remembered my ol' home town Southvale. Nice farmin' land, pretty decent climate, an' judgin' by reports an' rumors about this here whole region, settled down an' a'mos' rich. So I thought I'd come back.' Hammer's teeth gleamed white under the moon.

'Well, you always did love t' hear y'rself talk. Now suppose you say what your deal is.'

'Just this. The town's cut off from outside by ordinary means o' travel. Once we hold it, we can easy take care o' the outlyin' farms an' villages. *But* – you can see the gov'ment's been here. Few bugs in the crops, so somebody must'a been sprayin'. A jet overhead yestiddy. An' so on.'

They stirred uneasily. One muttered: 'I don't want nothin' to do with the gov'ment. They'll hang us f'r this.'

'If they can! They really ain't so strong. They ain't got aroun' to the South at all, 'cept f'r one 'r two visits. Way I figger it, there's only one gov'ment center to speak of, this town out in Oregon we heard about. We can find out 'zac'ly from the people we catch. They'll tell!

'Now look. The gov'ment must deal with Southvale, one way 'r 'nother. There ain't enough cars 'r roads, so they must use planes. That means one'll land in Southvale, sooner 'r later. The pilot steps out – an' we've got us a jet. I ain't forgot how to fly. Mebbe we can ferry a lot, fly to Oregon an' land at night near the house o' some big shot, mebbe even the President. The plane's pilot'll tell us what we need to know. Them jets just whisper along, an' anyway nobody expects air attack any more. We'll be just another incomin' plane if they do spot us.

'All right. We capture our big shot, an' find out from him where the atom bombs're kept. There must be some stockpiled near the city, an' our man'll make a front f'r us to get at 'em. If he ain't scared f'r himself, he's got a fam'ly. We set the bombs an' clear out. The city blows. No more gov'ment worth mentionin'. With what we've taken from the arsenals, we'll hold Southvale an' all this territory. We'll be bosses, owners – kings! Mebbe later we can go on an' conquer more land. There'll be no gov'ment to stop us.'

Hammer stood up. His eyes caught the moonlight in a darkly splendid vision – for he was, in his own estimate, not a robber. Hardened by pain and sorrow and the long bitter fight to live, he was more of a conqueror, an Alexander or Napoleon. He genuinely hoped to improve the lot of his own people, and as for others – well, 'stranger' and 'enemy' had been synonymous too long for him to give that side of it much thought now.

'No more hunger,' he breathed. 'No more cold an' wet, no more hidin' an' runnin' from a stronger gang, no more walkin' an' walkin' an' never gettin' nowheres. Our kids won't die before they're weaned, they'll grow up like God meant they should, free an' happy an' safe. We c'n build our own future, boys – I seem t' see it now, a tall city reachin' f'r the sun.'

His lieutenants stirred uneasily. After some ten years of association, they recognized their chief's strange moods but could not fathom them. His enormous ambitions were beyond the scope of minds focused purely on the day-to-day struggle for life. They were awed and half afraid. But even his enemies acknowledged Richard Hammer's skill and audacity and luck. This might work.

Their own ideas of a future went little beyond a house and a harem. But to smash the government was a cause worth giving life for. They associated it with the disaster, and thus with all their woes. And it was their enemy. It would kill them, or at least lock them up, for deeds done to survive when every man's hand was against them. It would surely never let them hold this green and lovely land.

Unless – unless!

The dog had been snuffling around the outlaw camp, a vague misshapen shadow in the fleeting moonlight. Now he howled once more and trotted down the ridge toward the dark silent mass of the town.

3

Alaric Wayne woke at the sound of scratching. For a moment he lay in bed, his mind still clouded with sleep. Moonlight streamed through the window to shimmer off the tumbled heaps of books and apparatus littering the room. Outside, the world was a black-and-white fantasy, unreal under the high stars.

Full wakefulness came. Alaric slid out of bed, went to the window, and leaned against the screen. It was his dog, scratching to get in. And – excited. He raised the screen and the animal jumped clumsily over the sill.

The dog whined, pulled at Alaric's leg, sniffed toward the south and shivered. The boy's great light eyes seemed to deepen and brighten, cold in the pouring moonlight; shadow-masked, his thin face was invisible, but its blankness slid into tight lines.

He had to – think!

The dog was warning him of danger from the south. But though the mutation shaping the canine brain had given it abnormal intelligence, he was still only a dog. He was not able to understand or reason above an elementary level. Three years ago, Alaric had noticed certain signs in the pup, and raised and trained it, and there was a curious partial rapport between them. They had cooperated before, to hunt or to avoid the wild dog packs on their long hikes.

But now there was danger. Men outside town, to the south, with hostile intentions. That was all the dog had been able to gather. It would have been enough for any normal human. But Alaric wasn't normal.

He stood trembling a little with effort, clenching his hands to his forehead as if to keep his spinning brain from explosion. What did it mean? What to do?

Danger was clear enough, and primitive instinct showed what to do. One ran from the bands of human boys when they intended to beat up a mutant, and hid. One skirted the spoor of wild dogs or of the bears beginning to spread since hunting diminished.

Only in this case – slowly, fighting itself, his mind spewed out the conclusion – in this case, one couldn't run. If the town went, so did all safety.

Think – *think!* There was danger, it couldn't be run from – what to do? His mind groped in a mist. There was nothing to grasp. Disjointed chains of logic clanked insanely in his skull.

Reason did not supply the answer, but instinct came, the instinct which would have taken over at once in the face of immediate peril and now finally broke through the storm of consciousness.

Why – it was so simple. Alaric relaxed, eyes widening with the sheer delightful simplicity of it. It was, really, as obvious as – why, it had all the elementariness of the three-body problem. If you couldn't run from danger you fought it!

Fighting, destruction . . . yes, something to destroy, but he would only have the newly reclaimed powerhouse to work with.

He scrambled frantically into his clothes. A glance at stars and moon told him, without the need for thought, how long till sunrise. Not long – and in his own way, he knew the enemy would attack just before dawn. He had to hurry!

He vaulted out the window and ran down the street, the dog following. It was a ribbon of moonlight, empty and silent. All the town's electrical and electronic equipment was stored at the powerhouse. It would be quite a while before the whole community had electricity again, but meanwhile the plant ran several important machines, charged storage batteries, and waited.

The building stood beside the river, a lighted window glowing in its dark bulk. Behind it, moonwhitened water rushed murmurously over the low dam. After the war there had been no time or parts to spare for the generators, and they had been plundered to repair the vital farm machinery, but recently the government had delivered what was necessary to start the hydroelectric turbines going again. It had occasioned a formal celebration in Southvale – another step up the ladder, after that long fall down.

Alaric beat on the door, yelling wordlessly. There came the sound of a scraping chair and the maddeningly slow shuffle of feet. Alaric jittered on the steps, gasping. No time, no time!

The door creaked open, and the night watchman blinked myopically at Alaric. He was an old man, and hadn't gotten new glasses since the war. 'Who're you, boy?' he asked. 'And what d'you want at this hour?'

Alaric brushed impatiently by him and made for the storeroom. He knew what he needed and what he must do with it, but the job was long and time was growing so terribly short.

'Here . . . hey, you!' The watchman hobbled after him, indignantly. 'You crazy mutie, what do you think you're doing?'

Alaric shook loose the clutching hand and gestured to his dog. The mongrel snarled and bristled, and the watchman stumbled back. 'Help!' It was a high, old man's yell. 'Help, burglar.'

Somehow words came, more instinctive than reasoned. 'Shut up,' said Alaric, 'or dog kill you.' He meant it.

The animal added emphasis with a bass growl and a vicious snap of fangs. The watchman sank into a chair, blood draining from his face, and the dog sat down to guard him.

The storeroom door was locked. Alaric grabbed a heavy wrench and beat down a panel. Tumbling into the room, he grabbed for what he needed. Wires – meters – tubes – batteries – *hurry, hurry!*

Dragging it out into the main chamber before the great droning generators, he squatted down, a tatterdemalion gnome, and got to work. The watchman stared through blurred and horrified vision. The dog regarded him steadily, with sullen malevolent hope that he would try something. It was embittering, to hate all the world save one being, because only that being understood.

False dawn glimmered over the land, touching houses and fields and glittering briefly off the swift-flowing river before deeper darkness returned. Hammer's gang awoke with the instant animal alertness of their kind, and stirred in the fog-drifting twilight. Their scant clothes were heavy with dew, they were cold and hungry – how hungry! – and they looked down at the moveless mass of their goal with a smoldering savage wish.

'Fair is the land,' whispered Hammer, 'more fair 'n land's ever been. The fields're green t' harvest, an' the fog runs white over a river like a polished knife – an' it's our land.' His voice rose, hard again: 'Joe, take twenty men an' circle north. Come in by the main road, postin' men at the edge o' town an' the bridge over the river, then wait in the main square. Buck, take your fifteen, circle west, an' come in the same time as Joe, postin' men outside town an' in that big buildin' halfway down Fifth Street – that's the machine shop, as I recall, an' I *hope* you can still read street signs. Then join Joe. The rest follow as straight north. Go as quiet as you can, slug 'r kill anyone you meet, an' be ready f'r a fight but don't start one. Okay!'

The two other groups filed down the hill and vanished into misty dusk. Hammer waited a while. He had previously divided the gang into bands assigned to his lieutenants, reserving the best men for the group directly under his command. He spoke to them, softly but with metallic speed:

'Accordin' t' what I remember o' Southvale, an' to what I seen elsewhere, they don't expect nothin' like this. There've been no bandits here f'r a long time, an' anyway they'd never think a gang had the skill an' self-control t' sneak through the fat lands farther south. So there'll be no patrol, just a few cops on their beats – an' too sleepy at this hour t' give us much trouble. An' nearly all the weapons're gonna be in the police station – which is what we're gonna capture. With guns, we'll control the town. But f'r Christ's sake, don't start shootin' till I say to. There may be armed citizens, an' they c'n raise hell with us 'nless we handle 'em right.'

A low mutter of assent ran along the line of haggard, bearded, fierce-eyed men. Knives and axes glittered in the first dim dawn-flush, bows were strung and spears hefted. But there was no rest-lessness, no uncontrollable lust to be off and into battle. They had learned patience the hard way, the past sixteen years. They waited.

Timing wasn't easy to judge, but Hammer had developed a sense for it which had served him before. When he figured the other bands were near the outskirts of town, he raised his hand in signal, slipped the safety catch on his gun, and started down the hill at a rapid trot.

The white mists rolled over the ground, but they needed nothing to muffle the soft pad of their feet, most bare and all trained in quietness. Grass whispered under their pace, a staked-out cow lowed, and a rooster greeted the first banners of day. Otherwise there was silence, and the town still slept.

They came onto the cracked pavement of the road, and it was strange to be walking on concrete again. They passed an outer zone of deserted houses. As Hammer had noticed elsewhere, Southvale had withdrawn into a compact defensive mass during the black years and not grown far out of it since. As long as there were no fortified outposts, such an arrangement was easy to overrun. Still, the gang was enormously outnumbered, and had to make up the difference with speed and ruthlessness. Hammer stopped at the edge of habitation, told off half a dozen men to patrol the area, and led the rest on toward the middle of town. They went more slowly now, senses drawn wire-taut, every nerve and muscle strained into readiness.

Hoofs clattered from a side street. Hammer gestured to a bowman, who grinned and bent his weapon. A mounted policeman came into view a few blocks down. He wasn't impressive, he had no sign of office except gun and tarnished badge, he was drowsy and eager to report to the station and then get home. His wife would have breakfast ready.

The bow twanged, a great bass throb in the quiet street. The rider pitched out of his saddle, the arrow through his breast, the astonishment on his face so ridiculous that a couple of gangmen guffawed. Hammer cursed; the horse had reared, neighed in panic, and then galloped down the avenue. The clattering echoes beat at the walls around like alarm-crying sentries.

A man stuck his head out of a window. He was still half asleep, but he saw the unkempt band outside and yelled – a choked gurgle it was, spitted on an arrow before it was properly born.

'Snagtooth an' Mex, get in that house an' silence anyone else!' rapped Hammer. 'You five –' he swept an arm in an unconsciously imperial gesture –'take care o' anybody else hereabouts who spots us. The rest *come on!*'

They ran down the street, disregarding noise but not making much anyway. The town had changed a lot, but Hammer remembered the general layout. The police station, he thought briefly and wryly, he knew very well – just about every Saturday night, in the old days.

They burst onto that block and raced for the station. There it was, the same square and solid structure, dingy now with years, the trimmings gone, but there were horses hitched before it and the door stood ajar.

Through the door! The desk sergeant and a couple of other men gaped blankly down the muzzle of Hammer's gun, then slowly their hands rose. Others of the gang poured down the short corridors beyond, into every room. There came yells, the clatter of feet, the brief sharp bark of a gun and the racket of combat.

Hoofs pounded outside. A pistol cracked, and one of Hammer's men, standing guard at the door, fell. Hammer himself jumped to the window, smashed the glass with his rifle butt, and shot at the half-dozen mounted police outside – returning from their beats, he thought, and alarmed at what they saw.

He had had little opportunity to practice. Shells were too scarce. His first shot went wild, the second hit a horse, the third also missed. But the riders retreated. They weren't such good shots either, though a couple of slugs whined viciously close, through the window and thudding into the wall beyond.

'Here, Dick!' His men were returning from the interior of the building, and they bore firearms, bore them as they would something holy and beautiful. 'Here, shootin' weapons!'

Hammer grabbed a submachine gun and cut loose. The troopers scattered, leaving their dead and wounded, and fled down the streets out of sight. Right toward the other outlaw divisions! Hammer laughed for joy.

'We got the whole station,' reported one of his men breathlessly. 'Bob got winged, an' I see they plugged Tony an' Little Jack. But the place is ours!'

'Yeah. Lock up these cops, take what guns an' horses you need, an' ride aroun' town. Herd ever'body down into the main square in the center o' town; shoot any that try to get away. Be careful, there'll be some trouble an' killin', but we don't have to be on the receivin' end o' any o' it. Mart, Rog, One-Ear, hold the station here an' look after our wounded. Sambo an' Putzy, follow me. I'm goin' t' the square now to take possession!'

4

There was noise in the street, running and stamping feet, shouts and oaths and screams. Now and then a gun spoke. Roderick Wayne gasped out of sleep, sweating. What a dream! Nightmare recollection of the black years –

No dream!

There was a tremendous kicking and beating on the door, and a voice bawling in an uncouth accent: 'Open up in there! Open up in the name o' the law!'

Laughter, like wolves yelping. A cry, suddenly broken off. Wayne jumped from his bed. Even then he was dimly surprised to find he wasn't shaking or gibbering in blind panic. 'Get Al, Karen,' he said harshly. 'Stay inside, in a back room. I've got to look into this.'

He stopped in the living room to get his own shotgun. It was a souvenir now, no cartridges left, but he had killed men with it once. *And must I go through that again? No – please no!*

Wood split and crashed, and a man leaped into the house over the fallen door. Wayne saw the pistol and dropped his own useless weapon. He remembered such ragged figures, the shaggy men whose triggers were always ready. The outlaws had returned.

'Smart,' nodded the gangman, ' 'nother sec 'n I'd 'a scragged you. Outside.'

'What . . . is . . . this?' Wayne's lips were stiff.

'Get out!'

Wayne went slowly, praying he could draw the bandit from the house. 'If it's loot you want,' he said, fighting to keep his voice level, 'I'll show you where the silver is.'

Another gangman entered. 'Ever'body out o' here?' he asked.

'I just got in,' said the first. 'I'll search it myself. Find y'r own house.' He turned on Wayne and slammed him in the stomach with a fist. 'Scram, you – down t' the main square!'

Retching, Wayne staggered back, and outside mostly by

chance. He leaned against the wall, sick and dizzy.

'Rod!'

He turned, sobbing his relief. Karen had just come around the side of the house, pale but with a calmness on her. 'Are you all right, Rod?' she breathed.

'Yeah . . . yeah . . . but you . . . how –?'

'I heard them talking and slipped out a window. But Rod – Al's gone.'

'Gone!' Briefly, Wayne was shaken afresh. Al – whatever the mutant was, Al was his son. Then realization came, and a huge thankfulness. 'He must have sneaked out too. He's all right. He knows how to run and hide – all mutant kids learn that.' His mind added darkly: *And in the next generation all human kids will have to learn it.*

'But us – Rod, what is this?'

Wayne started down the street as a bearded man jerked a thumb at him to be gone. 'Town's apparently captured,' he said.

'Outlaws –' Her fingers were cold on his arm. 'We have to run, dear! Get away!'

'Not much use, I'm afraid,' he answered hoarsely. 'This is the work of a well-disciplined group under a smart leader. They must have come up from the south, took us by surprise, over-powered the police – I recognized Ed Haley's pistol in that man's hand. Now they're rounding us up. I wasn't just shoved out, I was ordered to report to the main square. That suggests they're guarding all ways out.' He looked around him. 'Anyway, we can't escape now.'

They had fallen in with a band of citizens moving stunned and blank-eyed under outlaw guard. They must all have been routed from their beds, a few wore pajamas and the rest were naked. It made them look peeled, helpless to do anything but shuffle the way they were told. The invaders were having little trouble. They went from house to house, looking into each room and forcing the dwellers to the street. The work went fast.

Now and then there was fighting, short and sharp, ending in blow of club or knife or bullet. A couple of families with guns tried to hold off the enemy. Wayne saw fire arrows being shot into the roofs of those houses.

58

He shuddered and bent his head close to Karen's ear. 'We do have to get out as soon as we can,' he muttered. '*If* we can. They're disciplined now, but once the town is completely under control, you know what looting and raping and murdering will start.'

'They can't stay long,' she answered desperately. 'The government . . . this is an air route.'

'That's what I don't understand. They must know they can't remain, so why did they come here in the first place? Why not raid closer to home? Well – we'll have to see, that's all.'

The herd of humans entered the square and approached the monument in its center with the queer blind shuffle of cattle in a stockyard chute. There were other outlaw guards posted around the square and on the memorial. The monument was a granite shaft with a stone bench at its base, and seated on it was a man.

Wayne did not recognize the bearded giant, but Karen caught his arm again, breathing hard. 'It . . . Rod, it's Hammer. Richard Hammer!'

'Huh?'

'Don't you remember – the mechanic at the service station. We always used to get our work done there, and once when I smashed a fender on the car he fixed it so you wouldn't notice.'

The chief heard them. There weren't many prisoners in the square yet, and the early sun struck dazzling off Karen's hair. 'Why, it's Miz' Wayne,' he said, 'Howdy, Miz' Wayne.'

'H-h-h-hello.'

'Lookin' purtier'n ever, too. Wayne, you had all the luck.'

The mathematician shouldered his way forward, suddenly weak with a new fear. 'Hammer – what is this?' he got out.

'I'm takin' over Southvale. Meet the new mayor.'

'You –' Wayne swallowed. He choked down the rising panic and said in a level, toneless voice: 'I gather you've become chief of this gang and led it here for a raid. But you must know you can't get away with it. We're on an airline route. The government will know.'

Hammer smiled wearily. 'I've got that figgered. I intend t' stay here. I'm gatherin' all the folks to tell 'em t' be good, because we don't mind killin'. But if y're really interested –' He sketched his further plans.

'You're crazy!' cried Wayne. 'It's not possible.'

'A lot o' less possible things have happened. If you all, not too far north, felt safe, what about the gov'ment 'way out in Oregon? We'll do it!'

'But even if you can, Hammer, do you realize the government is all that's holding civilization together? You'd throw us back a thousand years.'

'So what?' Hammer spat. 'Wayne, don't you nor anybody else hand me none o' that crap 'bout law an' order an' humanity. You're fifteen years too late. You an' your kind made us outlaws, drivin' us away when we came starvin' to you, houndin' us south an' then sittin' back an' forgettin' about us. It's been hard, Wayne, fightin' and sickness an' hunger all them years. We had t' get hard ourselves, to stay alive.'

'You could have stuck it out in the north as we did,' said Wayne bitterly. 'You could have raised your own food free from most bandits.'

'Free only becuz so many people like us went south,' snapped Hammer. 'Nor was most o' us farmers, with land an' machinery an' experience. Anyway, you did drive us out when you all was strong. I ain't blamin' you. You had t' live. But it's our turn now, so shut up.' His eyes swung to Karen, and he smiled. It was a winter-cold smile, warmth and humor had long ago died in him. 'You, I'll be seein' more of,' he said. 'It's been so long –'

The square was filling up rapidly now. Some of the captives were still numb. Some wept or prayed or implored or tried to ingratiate themselves, some cursed and threatened, some retreated into silence. But – prisoners all. Captured, impotent, legitimate prey.

Hammer turned as an outlaw galloped up, thrusting his horse through the crowd without regard for their safety. 'What is it?' asked the chief, not anxiously. His victory was too tremendous.

'I dunno, boss, some trouble down by the river,' said the gangman. 'About half Joe's detail ain't showed up yet.'

'Hmmm? Must 'a found some likker.'

'Yeah – hey – *what's that?*'

Hammer turned. He couldn't see much sitting down. Huge and

shaggy and ablaze with his triumph, he sprang onto the bench and looked north along the street. He grinned, then laughed, then shouted with mirth. 'Lamp that, boys. Some crazy mutie – *look* at him!'

Wayne was so placed that he could also see down that street. His heart staggered, and for a moment he refused to believe. Then –

'*Alaric!*'

The boy was walking slowly and carrying something, a lunatic tangle of wires and coils and tubes, thrown together in the wildest haste. It was hooked to a reel of cable mounted on a mule's back, and the cable snaked behind, along the road – it must go clear to the powerhouse!

How had Al done it? The cable was sacrosanct, reserved for electrifying the airport. That apparatus, the invaluable parts in it – how had he gotten them? And why, why, why?

'Come on, kid,' shouted Hammer boisterously. 'What'cha got?'

Alaric approached closer. His thin features were set in concentration, his strange light eyes flashing like glacial ice, not a human gleam. He lifted his burden and twirled a pair of dials.

'May be a weapon,' said an outlaw uneasily and lifted his rifle.

'No!' Wayne yelled and made a clumsy lunge. Hammer swept one long arm in a careless blow and sent him to the ground.

The gangman squeezed the trigger of his rifle but never completed the motion. He was dead before he could. Wayne, sprawled on his back and looking up through a fog of horror, saw the man's body explode.

It went up in a white burst of steam, a crash of rending bone and tissue and a brief glare of incandescence. The rifle flying from him glowed cherry red, blowing up as its cartridges detonated, and he himself became a column of greasy smoke. Before the pieces had fallen, something had swept the outer edges of the square, and where the guards had stood were steam and black fumes and shredded flesh.

The crowd yelled, a single beast cry half of terror and half of triumph, and swept down on the remaining gangmen. It became a riot, where the outlaw numbers were too few and they were ripped in pieces.

Hammer roared as the mob raged toward him. A horse reared as

61

its rider was yanked from the saddle. Two slugging blows, and Hammer had cleared a way to the mount. He sprang up on its back, howling, and the townsfolk scattered from his charge.

Almost, he made it. He was on the edge of the square when a man whose brother had been killed made a long jump and grabbed the horse's bridle – grabbed it, and hung on till a dozen men held the gang boss secured.

Not many of the outlaws escaped. The rest, such as were not simply kicked and beaten to death in the riot, were hanged that afternoon. Nobody was in a mood for jury trials. Hammer asked not to be blindfolded, and they granted him that much. To the end, he stood looking out over the sun-glittering river, the rolling wooded hills, and the fair broad land green to harvest.

Wayne took no part in the executions. He had other things to think about.

5

After the celebrations, the parades and parties and speeches, the reorganization and the tightening of defenses, there was a rather grim conference in Roderick Wayne's home. He and Karen were there, seated before the fire, and Alaric sat opposite them, nervous and bewildered. A government representative was present, a lean man who looked older than he was, Robert Boyd by name and roving Presidential agent by profession. In the corner, half hidden by shadow, lay the hairy trollshape of the dog, watching with sullen red eyes.

'You've heard the official account,' said Wayne. 'Alaric, a mutant *idiot savant*, invented and built a weapon to defeat the outlaws. He's been made much of, and nobody pays any attention to Pop Hansom – he's the powerhouse watchman, and was rather rudely treated. Geniuses are expected to be eccentric.'

'Well,' said Boyd, smiling a little, 'a lot of them are.'

'Not that eccentric. If so many people hadn't died, I'd say this was a good thing. It taught us not to be complacent and careless. More important, it indicated that mutants can serve society as talented members.' Wayne's eyes were bleak. 'Only you see, Al didn't behave like a genius. He behaved like a low-grade imbecile.'

'Inventing that –'

'Yes, going all around Robin Hood's barn, committing violence and theft, working like a slave, risking his neck, all to build that weapon and use it. But he told me his dog warned him hours ahead of time. Certainly he was at the powerhouse well before the raid. Don't you see, we could have been ready for the outlaws, we could have stood them off, driven their ill-armed force away with no loss to us *if Alaric had merely gone to the police with that warning.*'

Thunderstruck, Boyd swung his eyes to meet the blue vacancy of Alaric's. 'Why . . . didn't you?' he asked, very softly.

The boy stared, slowly focusing his mind and vision. His face twisted with effort. He . . . his father had told him the day before . . . what was it now? Yes – 'I . . . didn't . . . think of it,' he fumbled.

'You didn't think of it. It just never occurred to you.' Boyd turned dazedly to Wayne. 'As long as you've said it yourself, I agree – *idiot savant.*'

'No,' said Karen gently. 'No, not in any ordinary sense. Such a person is feeble-minded in all but one respect, where he is a genius. I used to teach school, and know a little psychology. Yesterday I gave Al some tests I'd worked out. Science, mechanical skill, reading speed, comprehension – in too many respects, he's a genius.'

'I give up,' said Boyd. 'What *is* he, then?'

'A mutant,' said Karen.

'And . . . this weapon?'

'Alaric tried to tell me, but we couldn't understand each other,' said Wayne. 'And the thing itself burned out very quickly in use. It's just fused junk now. From what I could gather, though, and by deduction on that basis, I think it projected an intense beam of highly complex wave form to which one or more important organic compounds in the body resonate. They disintegrated, releasing their binding forces. Or perhaps it was body colloids that were destroyed, releasing terrific surface energies. I'm just as glad I don't know. There are too many weapons in the world.'

'Mmmm – officially I can't agree with you, but privately I do. Anyway, the inventor is still here – the genius.'

'It takes more than genius,' said Wayne. 'It just isn't possible for any human being to sit down and figure such a thing out in detail. All the facts are available, in handbooks and texts and papers – quantum mechanics, circuit characteristics, physical constants. But even if he knew exactly what he was after, the greatest genius in the world would have to spend months or years in analytical thought, then more time in putting all those facts together into the pattern he was after. And even then he wouldn't know it all. There'd be a near infinitude of small factors interacting on each other that he couldn't allow for. He'd have to build a model and experiment, the engineering process known as getting the bugs out.'

Wayne cleared his throat and resumed after a pause: 'In his incoherent way, Alaric told me his only difficulty was to figure out what to do to meet the danger. All he could think of was to make some kind of weapon. But he spent only a few minutes working out the design of that devil's engine, and his first model was as nearly perfect as his inadequate tools and materials permitted. He *knew* how to make it.'

With an effort, Boyd relaxed. He couldn't look at that small, big-headed figure in the armchair. The ancient human dread of the unknown was too strong in him. He asked slowly: 'What's the answer, then?'

'Karen and I think we've figured it out, and what little Al can tell us seems to confirm our idea. But I'll have to explain it in a roundabout way. Tell me, how does a person think?'

'Think? Why . . . well . . . by logic. He follows a logical track.'

'Exactly!' said Wayne. 'A track. He thinks in chains of logic, if under that we include everything from mathematics to emotional experience. Premise to conclusion. One thing leads to another, one step at a time.

'Physics and math have been able to make their great strides because they deal, actually, with the simplest concepts, which are artificially simplified still further. Newton's three laws of motion, for instance, assume that no force beyond the one set being considered is acting on a given body; and the members of this set can be considered one at a time, as if they acted independently. We never really observe such a case. There is always friction, gravitation, radiation, or some other disturbing influence. What saves physics is that these externals are usually negligibly small.'

It felt strangely good, warm, to be lecturing again: 'Take a particular case. You know the two-body problem in astronomy? Given two bodies of known mass, velocity, and distance from each other, and the laws of motion and gravitation, to find their position at any past or future time. It was solved long ago. But the three-body problem is quite another story. Right away, with three sets of interaction, it becomes so complex that as far as I know there's never been any general solution, and only a few special ones. As for the n-body problem –

'Now in the biological sciences, including psychology and sociology, you can't simplify. You have to consider the whole. A living organism is an incredibly complex set of interactions, beginning, probably, on the subatomic level and going on up to the entire universe, from which the organism cannot be separated either. You *can't* apply our single-track analytic methods to such a case. The result is, of course, that aside from a few statistical regularities, those sciences are almost purely empirical, sociology hardly deserving the name. If, to use an old illustration, I want to tackle the three-body problem, I can and will start with the special case where one of them has zero mass. But suppose I were making an analysis of the influence of Pan-Asiatic foreign policy on American domestic affairs before the war. I could certainly not ignore the converse case, or the existence of other countries. It's a fluid web of interactions. I'd have to consider them all simultaneously – which no existing symbology can do. Any results I got would be qualitative, nonmathematical, nonpredictive – you see?'

'I think I do,' nodded Boyd. 'Of course, people can think of two or more things at once.'

'That's different,' said Karen. 'That's a case of divided attention, each branch of the mind following its single track. It's normal enough, though carried to extremes it becomes schizophrenia.'

'You get what I'm driving at,' went on Wayne. 'Our subhuman and human ancestors didn't need to see the world as a whole. They were only concerned with immediate surroundings and events. So we never evolved the ability to think of an entire entity. On a childish level, how many bricks can you visualize in your imagination, side by side and not quite touching? I believe the ordinary human limit is half a dozen. Alaric says he can see any number, and I believe him. He's a mutant.'

'Some different brain structure,' said Karen. 'The X-rays don't show it, so it's probably a very subtle matter of cells or . . . what-you-call-'ems . . . colloids, or of organization.'

'Al didn't have to think, in our ordinary sense of the word, to design that weapon,' said Wayne. 'His extensive knowledge of scientific principles and data coordinated in his mind to show him. Well, if my guess is right, then the cells of human bodies are resonant to a particular wave form. And at once he knew all the factors he'd need to generate that wave. It wasn't reasoned, as we reason, though it was thought – to him, thought on a very elementary, almost primitive level. Yet he didn't think of merely warning people.'

'I get it,' said Boyd. 'Humans think in chains. He thinks in networks.'

'Yes, that's about the size of it.'

'Do you think . . . we . . . can ever do it?'

'Hmmm –' Wayne rubbed his chin. 'I don't know. Since intelligence seems to depend on upbringing among normal humans, whereas genius and feeble-mindedness seem more nearly independent to training and are hereditary, one might argue that they are both mutations. Some people seem to have had a degree of the network-thinking ability – like Nikola Tesla, I read a biography of him once. The fact that Al is the son of a mathematician, who does deal with complexities, is suggestive. After all, no mutation ever created a totally new characteristic. It would have to create a whole new set of genes for that. A mutation is a greater or lesser modification of an existing trait.

'The point I'm making is that humans naturally think in straight lines, but some sort of network, total-considering logic has been developed. The semanticists have their nonelementalistic principle. In math, we only add in special cases, the rest of the time we integrate; and we have our generalized calculi of vectors and tensors. *But* – it doesn't come naturally. It's been worked out slowly and painfully, through many centuries.

'To Al, it's the natural way to think; but since like most mutations, it involves a loss elsewhere, the simple straightforward logic of humans is unnatural to him. And he's just a kid, and probably not a genius anyway – merely an ordinary network thinker – so he hasn't seen the principles of that logic, any more than a human his age sees the principle of nonelementalism. I'd say, offhand, that each type of mind can learn the other type of thought, but not comprehend or apply it on its higher levels.'

'There's another thing,' put in Karen. Her eyes held a light which hadn't been there for a long time. 'Rod just said it. With the proper training, Al should be able to learn logic, at least enough to understand and communicate. His kind of thought is not adapted to the simple problems of everyday life, but he can be taught to handle those, as we teach human children unnatural things like algebra and physics. Maybe . . . maybe, then, be can teach us something.'

Boyd nodded again. 'It's certainly worth the attempt,' he said. 'We have psychiatrists and other specialists at the capital. If we'd known before that you were a mathematician, Dr. Wayne, we'd have asked you to join the new science center. Consider yourself invited as of now. And if we and Alaric can come to understand each other – why, you may even get your biological and sociological math. Then we may be able to build the first sane civilization in history.'

'I hope so,' murmured Wayne. 'I certainly hope so. And thanks, Boyd.'

He smiled tiredly. 'By the way, Karen, you have your superman there. The highest genius, in his way, that the world ever saw. If he hadn't had some kind of protection to grow up in and, now, to teach him the elements of thought, he'd never have lived. I'm afraid this particular kind of superman isn't much of a survivor type.'

'No,' whispered Karen. 'Nor human.' Her hand ruffled the boy's hair, and he smiled shyly up at her. 'But he's our son.'

The Children of Fortune

Now are we come
to the house of the king.
Bad luck has made us
thralls at the millstone.
Gravel gnaws our feet,
we freeze above,
but have peace to work –
and woe with Frodhi.

Now hands shall hold
the hardened spears
and the reddened weapons.
Waken, Frodhi!
Waken, Frodhi! –
if thou wilt listen
to our songs of war
and stories of old.

Fire see I burning
on eastern beaches,
signs which watch and
warn of battle.
A host is coming,
hither it hastens
to burn the houses,
the home of Frodhi.

Thou shalt be thrust
from Leidhra's throne,
from ruddy rings

and the quern of riches.
Grip harder, maiden,
about the mill's handle,
for now we are grinding
blood on the ground.

  – *The Song of Grotte*
  (Anon., ca. 10th century A.D.)

1

The arrow came from a screen of brush, so fast that Collie was not aware of it until it had gone by. Woodsman's reflex sent him leaping from the thing as it flashed, and the steel head thudded home into a tree.

His second movement was upward. Twenty feet overhead, a branch was a blur of leaves and sunlight. His hands caught it, clung, and he chinned himself and threw a leg over. Crouched there, he drew a long gasp and looked down.

Two men came out of the thicket and stared wildly about them. They were clad in tattered old levis, roughly tanned buckskin shirts, and their feet were bare on the soft forest floor. One was an Indian, a big gray-haired man, too old to be a mutie; the other was younger, perhaps sixteen, and had only three fingers to his hands. He grasped the bow, the Indian held a spear, and both had knives.

There was no other way out of this, and no time to be afraid. Collie sprang again, drawing his shortsword even as he fell. He hit with a force that jolted through his legs and rattled his teeth. Stabbing out, he caught the bowman in the stomach.

The youth screamed, dropping his weapon and clutching blindly at his belly. His comrade roared and struck out with the spear. It tore Collie's shirt and furrowed along his shoulder. He yanked the sword free and leaped back ten feet. The Indian's eyes grew wide. He hefted the spear, holding it before him as if for defense. Collie danced around him, seeking a way in. The Indian snarled, braced himself, and threw the shaft. It was a viciously fast movement, the head almost nailed Collie before he could spring.

'Ya-a-ah!' He jumped closer, crouched low and stabbing the way he had been taught. The Indian drew his knife and thrust

73

underhanded. Then Collie had beaten down his guard and gone to work. It was not pretty.

Breathing hard, Collie withdrew his blade and stood bent over two dead men. His blood was loud in his ears. Looking around, straining, he could discern only the rustle of leaves and the far-off harsh laughter of a jay. Fragments of sky showed through the forest roof, incredibly blue against its green. The woods were all shadow, speckled with sun, full of murmurs and dimness. No one else – nothing.

Slowly, Collie plunged his sword into the ground to clean it. A thoughtfulness grew within him. It was – how long? Three years? – since there'd been outlaw trouble. Were these only a pair of strays, or was there a larger band somewhere? No way of telling, now when they sprawled staring sightlessly and flies were already on their wounds.

Collie shivered. He'd never killed men before. Never wanted to, either. He wondered if he ought to be sick or something.

No. Why should he? They were dead meat, there on the ground. Soon the earth would claim them and only the white bones would be left. They were nothing to him – a danger, a pest, *outlaws*. What counted now was letting the town know.

He picked up the weapons and studied them. Crude things, cold-forged out of steel scrap; the bow and arrows weren't bad, but they had better in town. Well, the blacksmith could rework the metal, he'd pay a cent or two for it. Collie stuck the knives in his belt, alongside his own, threw the quiver across his back, and picked up the spear. His free hand clashed his sword back to its sheath.

He'd only been out for a walk, with some vague notion of trying to find the catamount's den. It had been raiding sheepfolds for the past month, eluding all attempts to catch or kill it. Too damn smart for an ordinary animal – it must be mutie. Well, that could wait now.

Turning from the dead men, Collie broke into a rapid trot homeward. He had ten miles or so to cover – about an hour's travel. The woods closed in around him and he was alone again.

He went softly, senses alert. There might well be others skulking around. No great need to fear them: given any kind of warning, he could get away faster than pursuit.

The forest was tall and old, reaching farther along the western slopes of the Wind River Range than Collie had ever gone. He followed the slanting ground northwesterly, toward home. The thick mould underfoot muffled his passage, the brush barely whispered as he parted it. Sunlight and shadow blent into confusion here, you couldn't see far and yet it was like standing in the middle of forever. A vault of branches rustled high overhead.

Collie loped without breathing hard. He was a tall young man, twenty-four years old – or maybe twenty-three or twenty-five, nobody was quite sure. From the outside he didn't look like a mutie. The homespun clothes hid his otherness, and the thin brown face was human enough. But when you looked closer, you saw that he was a bit too short in the body, a little too broad and deep in the chest, and entirely too long in the leg. It wasn't enough to be a misproportion, but it gave him a coltish look.

A rabbit bolted from his path. Collie didn't have time to see him well, but those weren't rabbit ears: they were big and round, more like a mouse's. And had there been a tail at all?

Nothing important. Maybe half the animals and people you saw were mutie, though only among humans were you likely to find a really deformed one. The bad cases among animals didn't live long enough. It did not occur to Collie that his standards of 'real' deformity were no older than his own generation.

Emerging on a long slope that spilled down toward a distant river, Collie crossed three miles of open land. There'd been a forest fire here once. The oldtimers said there were some enormous fires in the years after the war, when there was no one to fight them. The forests had shrunk, though they were starting to come back now. They didn't seem crowded, though – so few people around. The gray line of a highway showed halfway down the slope, crumbled, overgrown, pieces bitten out of it by avalanches. Collie wondered what it had been like before the war. He couldn't imagine it as full of cars, like the oldtimers said.

The burned area was covered with new growth. Collie noticed a sapling which had escaped his eyes before. It was a funny one, all long willowy fronds and ferny leaves. He went through a patch of clover without stopping to look for four-leaved ones as he'd often done in younger days; even if there'd been time, they were getting just too damn common.

The farmlands started on the other side of the burned section. Collie struck out down the narrow trail between fields of grain. He had covered a good mile before he realized what was wrong. This was cultivating time, but nobody was out in the communal fields.

Nobody!

The outlaws –

His heart stumbled with him, and then he burst into a run. The land slipped by him, sun-flooded, wind-whispering, his moccasins thudded softly on the dirt and somewhere a bird was singing. He breathed hard, not for air but because he was frightened.

God in Heaven, suppose it was a real outlaw attack? Suppose they had fallen on the town? There were stories enough of that from the old days – pillaging, burning, a scream of children drowned by barking laughter, dead men staring at the sky, fire and smoke and ruin. *No!*

He topped a ridge and looked wildly down toward the village. It lay quiet under the sun, a sprawl of paintless houses, a few horses hitched to posts and wagons. Collie's breath sobbed back into his lungs.

But where was everybody?

Hurrying down, he entered the outskirts. The stockade had been removed years ago, but the outlying houses were still supposed to be defensive posts. There was no one in them, no one in the street beyond. A cat yawned at him as he went by. It had two tails.

As he neared the center of town, he heard the noise, feet, voices, excitement, but not panic. So everybody was in the market square for some reason, and he'd come back in time for the fun. Collie smiled shakily and rounded the last building.

The broad open plaza was jammed, all the town's three or four hundred people were there. It was too familiar a sight to register on Collie's mind – men in clothes like his own, mostly bearded, a few carrying guns but the rest armed with knives and shortswords; women in dresses and clumsily made hats; children in whatever clothes or lack of them there happened to be. It was on the thing they surrounded that Collie's eyes focused.

A big metal shape, blinding in hot sunlight – long vanes reaching out over the heads – a helicopter! By God, a helicopter!

Collie grabbed the arm of a fifteen-year-old. 'What's this, Joe?' he asked. 'What's goin' on?'

Joe faced around to him. 'Hi, Collie,' he said breathlessly. 'Where you been? Gee, they been lookin' all over for you.'

'For *me*?' Collie drew back a little. 'You're kiddin'!'

'Yeah, you, nobody else. It's from Oregon, Collie, it's a guv'mint copter, an' they said they was lookin' for the runner they'd heard tell of, an' –'

Collie didn't wait any longer, but began shoving through the crowd. Joe looked wistfully after him, and wheeled his primitive chair around in search of a better view. Joe had been born without legs.

2

There were two men in the copter. The pilot was a lean, quiet young fellow in uniform, an automatic holstered at his belt; the other was some forty years of age, though he looked older, and in civilian dress. It was not too strange that so many of the townspeople should admire and wonder at their clothes more than anything else – aircraft were not uncommon, flying far overhead. But stuff such as this, the denseness and fineness of it, the color and cut and invisible seams, that was wholly new to the young and like a dear buried memory to the older. Only tattered fragments of pre-war cloth were left hereabouts.

The sun was sliding down under the mountains, and candles were beginning to glow in windows. A breeze wandered forth with the tall shadows, low and sad out of endless woods and ranges, bearing with it the faint hoot of an owl and the long-drawn wail of a wild dog. Night and quiet came swiftly up here.

Boss Johnson's home was, obviously, the only one for such distinguished visitors. A fire burned large in the dining room hearth, crackling and sputtering, throwing its restless light on a few pictures and skins and such furniture as there was. The older children scurried about, serving dinner – fish, soup, venison, potatoes, black bread, butter, and the town's best hard cider. The Boss' wife was a large pale woman, subdued in the burly, bearded presence of her husband. Collie felt too shy to say much either; he sat uncomfortably in his holiday clothes, on the edge of his chair, and listened to the Boss rumble on.

'Yep, gents, we ain't got it so bad. There was hard years right after the war, like everybody else had, I reckon. Not many was left in this village. Most of the folks livin' here now drifted in later, from other places. There was a few enemy sojers, even, who'd been wanderin' around f' years. They turned out to be pretty good people, once you got to know 'em. We or-gay-nized, fought the outlaws, rounded up wild stock, started plantin' again, grazin', huntin' – *you* know. Had to make damn near all our own stuff, still make most of it, though we do some tradin' with other sections too. There's been troubles, crop failures, one year there was some sickness damn near wiped out our sheep – was that one o' the war sicknesses, you think?'

'No, probably not,' said the government envoy, Temple. 'Those didn't last very long. Some mutated form of another disease, I imagine. We get them all the time.'

'Well, anyway, this ain't such a bad little town we got,' said Johnson. 'We're pretty happy, though o' course we need a lot o' things yet. We take care of our muties, too – more'n I can say for some places,' he added darkly.

Temple sighed. 'I know. Infanticide. Anti-mutant mobs. Local pogroms. It never helps. Mutants keep right on being born. It's in the race by now. We'll never be rid of it.'

'Reckon not,' said Johnson. 'We can find somethin' for ever-'body to do. Stupid muties dig, work in the fields, cut wood. Crippled ones is weavers an' carpenters an' so on. We got one young girl born without eyes, but she's the smartest tailor you ever did see.'

'Good for you,' said Temple.

'Oh, it ain't me entirely,' said Johnson, puffing himself out a bit. 'We ain't like some places I could name. We got a dem-*moc*-cracy here. Me, the Boss, I'm just sort of judge an' chairman o' town meetin's, an' in case o' war I got to lead. That's all. By the way, Collie – uh, Jim,' he added, 'I wouldn' worry about them savages you met today. I sent out scouts, an' they say there's no sign of a war party. Must just'a been a couple o' tramps.'

Temple smiled wryly. 'We nearly had our trip for nothing, Mr. Collingwood,' he said. 'If you'd been killed out there –'

Collie shuffled his feet and looked down at the table.

'You still ain't said just what you want our boy for,' said Johnson. 'I was hopin' you'd come to 'stablish some reg'lar connections with the guv'mint. Trade, a airline – *you* know. Hell, we don't even get to vote.'

'And you don't pay taxes either,' said Temple. 'Which are pretty steep these days. Lot of reconstruction to do, education, re-integration. We'll get around to you when we can, Boss, but meanwhile I think you're just as well out of civilization.'

The village chief's small eyes rested thoughtfully on the other man. He wasn't stupid. 'I got a hunch there's more to it than that,' he said, slowly.

'Well, yes, there is,' said Temple. 'I can tell you, because you've had an enlightened policy toward mutants, but I'd rather the word didn't spread too far.'

'Sure, go ahead.' Johnson took an apple off the dessert plate and bit into it. 'Try one o' these, why don't you? Mutie stock – got a kind of chestnut flavor.'

'The fear and revulsion aroused by the mutants has led to some pretty ghastly episodes,' said Temple quietly. 'Lynchings, murders – well, you know the story, I'm sure. We've got to stop that, but we just haven't the men or the resources to police the continent. We have to concentrate on building up our industry in the most promising areas, and more or less let the rest go for the time being. There are literally thousands of primitive communities like your own, from the Yukon to the Rio Grande. They weren't hit directly by the war, but the breakdown of industry and transportation threw them back on their own resources, and they've had to return to a natural economy. And one which is still, to some extent, menaced by roving bandit gangs, so that they have to maintain armed strength as well. We could do more for them, even now, than we are, but we're holding back, leaving most of them on their own for several years more.'

There was a moment's silence. The fire crackled loudly in the room. 'How come?' asked Johnson.

'Because of the anti-mutant hysteria and killing. As I said, we – the government – can't stop it everywhere. But a primitive community, threatened from outside, needs all its members. Before long, it learns from experience that it can't discriminate, because it needs every pair of hands to work and fight. Therefore, after a while, the mutants become accepted.'

Johnson rumbled something in his throat. He didn't like what had been said – in some ways, it was humiliating. 'If you're through eatin', gents,' he muttered, 'let's move into the livin' room.'

The house had been a large and gracious one before the war, but the attrition of time had gaunted it. The walls were bare and splotchy, the floor creaked underfoot, the furniture was old and shabby, the repairs were unskillful. The one truly good item was a chair of recent manufacture. Temple paused to admire it. 'Craftsmanship,' he said.

'One-eyed Bill did that,' answered Johnson, somewhat mollified. 'A mute – born with just one good eye – but he can sure handle wood.'

His hostility was quite dissolved when Temple offered him a cigar. He held it reverently. 'Tobacco!' he whispered. 'Ain't seen none in ten, twelve years. An' that was lousy stuff.'

'This isn't prewar quality, I'm afraid,' smiled Temple.

He turned to Collie, who sat shyly in a corner. 'But we came about you, Mr. Collingwood,' he went on.

Collie's face felt hot, but he made himself meet Temple's eyes. 'What for?' he asked.

'It's a long story,' said Temple. 'But we'd like to take you with us to Taylor – the capital.'

'*Huh?*'

'If you want to go,' added Temple hastily.

'Bu-bu-but –'

'Look, Mr. Collingwood, I understand you're a mutant with amazing powers.'

'Oh, no,' mumbled Collie, looking at the floor and twisting his hands together. 'I can run faster'n anybody else, maybe, an' jump better, an' hold my breath longer. That's all.'

'That's plenty! You don't have any troubles, do you? Anything wrong?'

When Collie didn't answer, Johnson said: 'No. He's a lucky boy, he is.'

'You don't realize how lucky,' said Temple. 'About seventy-five percent of human births since the war have been mutant in one way or another, and even though the radioactivity that caused it is dying down now, the percentage of such births is going up instead of down. That's because more and more mutated genes are finding their complements as the mutants themselves reach the age of reproduction – well, never mind that.

'The point is that a large proportion of the mutations have been harmless, or at least not a serious handicap – just meaningless deformities. A somewhat larger proportion have been unfavorable in greater degree. That's only natural, of course. A random change is much more likely to be for the worse instead of the better.

'In fact, harmless and bad mutations account for practically all the new births. The number of truly favorable, valuable ones is infinitesimal. Maybe half a million since the war, throughout the world, maybe even less. Mr. Collingwood has one of them. There are damn few people who have others.'

'All right,' said Collie hoarsely. 'What of it?'

'You'll excuse a few personal questions, I'm sure,' said Temple. 'Do you have any dependents here, close relatives – anything to make you stay?'

'No,' said Collie. 'Got no family. My mother died years ago. She had a kid, an' the mutie thing was too big, an' –' He stopped, his fists closing.

'I'm sorry,' whispered Temple.

'Dad got drowned one spring when the river was in flood,' went on Collie. 'I got two sisters, they're both married now. Nobody else.'

'Women are still scarce around here,' added Boss Johnson. 'Ain't easy f'r a young man to get a wife. I been sort o' thinkin' I'd give Collie my Janet, she's born human, but she's only thirteen now an' it's better to wait a couple years.'

'But nothing binding, right?' said Temple. 'You could come with us if you wanted to.'

'Why, I reckon so,' answered Collie. He was beginning to overcome his timidity. 'But what for?'

'We want to get all the good mutants we can together,' said Temple. 'We don't like them running around where any accident could kill them, the way you nearly died today, when the race needs their heredity so desperately.'

Collie flushed, Johnson slapped his thigh and guffawed. 'Settin' you out to stud, hey, boy?' he cried.

'No, no.' Temple frowned. 'Nothing like that. You'd have a home given you, education if you want it – be an ordinary citizen, free to leave anytime you wished. Of course, I can't promise you that till the doctors have looked you over, but I'm sure you'll pass. We can talk about it later if you're interested.'

Collie looked up. It was only now beginning to grow in him, what this meant.

Johnson cleared his throat. 'I got a boy,' he said diffidently. 'Six years old, about, but smart's a whip. Real smart. 'Course, he got a funny heart, gets pains in it, but he's real smart. Your doctors could mebbe –'

'I'm sorry,' said Temple with gentleness. 'That isn't what we're looking for. But we'll be sending medical missions around to this district spoon.'

Collie didn't hear. He couldn't, above the wild clamor in his ears. Taylor – the capital of North America – civilization – the world!

The *world*!

3

The mountains slipped away beneath them, the tall and lonely Tetons, Jackson Hole, the Bitterroot Range, deep valleys and shining rivers, forests green and fair, and then the farmlands which reached beyond sight. Collie had to pull his eyes away from the country below.

The cabin was full of the engine-purr, not loud, but everywhere, in your ears and muscles and bones. He had been told they were traveling a hundred miles an hour or better – fantastic, meaningless figure – but he found it hard to believe, the land changed so slowly down there. 'When'll we be in Taylor?' he asked.

'Oh, some hours yet,' answered Temple. 'Toward evening, I guess.'

'I –' Collie stirred restlessly. He wasn't used to such cramped quarters, though he could sit motionless for a whole day in a blind. 'All that way for me?'

'Sure,' said Temple. 'You're more valuable than you know, Collie, if you want me to call you that.'

'Ever'body else does.'

'Well, then, I'm Bob, eh?'

Collie shook his head, a little dazedly. It still seemed like a dream. This time yesterday he was setting out after a catamount.

'How'd you find me?' he asked, forcing down his awkwardness. 'It's a big country, an' we never had much to do with outsiders.'

'Oh, word gets around,' said Temple. 'Hunters, traders, or the better sort of tramp – they spread gossip. Without other communication, your kind of people are always interested in gossip.

'We, that is, the survey teams, are always out, visiting selected communities, studying them, talking to people – trying to learn as much as we can. The government has to know, for a number of reasons. One reason is just so we can find out what help you need most, and give it to you. But the teams keep their ears especially open for stories about favorable mutations. When they hear any such tale, they track it down at once.'

Temple sighed. 'Not many of them are true. Stories get distorted, or wishful thinking blends in, or somebody has just been lying. But every once in a while, we do find a really good case. Like yours.'

Collie sat quiet for a little, too embarrassed to talk further. Then, to change the subject, he asked: 'What's it like out there? Where you are, I mean. The guv'mint.'

Temple laughed. 'That would take a long time to answer, Collie. We've got a union of all North America now – except Mexico, anyway, which wanted to stay independent. Officially, you're a citizen too, even if we haven't been able to do much about your people yet. It's not such a bad place to live, nowadays. There's enough to eat, and we're turning out some fine new machines, and there's travel and communication everywhere. It's a free country too, though maybe not as free as it once was. But I think you'll like it.'

'But how 'bout the rest o' the world? What's it like for them?'

Temple reached into a cabinet and got out a book. 'Here are some maps,' he said. 'Look, here's a map of the world. This is North America, and –'

'I know,' said Collie, a trifle miffed. 'We got a school to home. I can read an' write, some, an' they taught joggerphy too.'

'Yes,' said Temple musingly, half to himself, 'literacy dies hard. There were too many books around, even after the war. Knowledge wasn't lost, though in places like yours it couldn't be applied.'

'Books don't say too much,' Collie told him. 'Not much we can use, like how to make a gun. Handiest damn book in town was somethin' called a Boy Scout manual. Most o' what we use, we had to figger out f'r ourselves.'

'I know. It was that way everywhere. Civilization got too far from the basics, it turned too many of its members into specialized cogs that couldn't exist once the great machine had broken down. Sometimes I wonder if the cycle of wars that ended with the mutants didn't express some deep unconscious hatred of the whole thing. But I'm daydreaming now, Collie. You wanted to know about the world.

'Look, Latin America is coming back like us, though not in the same form. Brazil, Argentina, Venezuela, and Mexico have absorbed just about all the other states, though their governments are often shadowy things. We won't have to reckon with them till they get a lot better organized, and a lot more industry; and then we hope they'll be our friends.

'Now, here in the Pacific, Australia and New Zealand are still going concerns, they weren't too badly hit in the first place. They more or less run the South Pacific Ocean. Malaya dominates the archipelago and the Indian Ocean.

'The Near East is still pretty anarchic, though Turkey has taken over most of it. Territorially, it's almost a revival of the old Ottoman empire, with a slice of southern Russia added, though the Turks run it better now than they did once. North Africa is partly Turkish, partly independent Arab and Berber states. Barbaric. South Africa was taken over by the negroes, who're building up a state reaching from Capetown to the Congo. All of this is still technologically backward, little heard from.

'Europe is a tottering ruin, most of it lost to barbarism. There's a Russian state, bordering on the Baltic, but it's pretty feeble, and squeezed in between Ukraine and Siberia. Big chunks of India have been taken over by Afghan warlords, the rest has gone back to something timeless. China is split into warring provinces, most of it no further along than your own people, Collie.

'Now here's Siberia.' Temple's face and voice harshened. 'It set itself up as independent when the old Russian government vanished. Not being too badly hurt, and having a certain amount of industry, an energetic population, and plenty of natural resources, it came back fast – as fast as we, if not more so. It's annexed Manchuria, you can see, and Mongolia and Korea; Japan is its puppet, as are several of the North Chinese states. We don't know a great deal about it, international communication is still pretty slim, but it's a hardboiled outfit, and its Khan – well, you can learn about that later on.'

Collie subsided. He hadn't followed all of what was said, though he got the drift. The vision of a planet in ruin was not saddening to him, he'd grown up with it. But he began for the first time to realize just how big the world was, how big and strange and threatening.

He wished he could turn around and go back, bury himself in his mountains and woods, forget the world that roared outside. But it was too late. Already it was too late . . .

Taylor wasn't large by the old standards; even today, there were bigger cities. But to Collie it was enormous, a reaching, rearing vastness of buildings, rushing steel streams of traffic, spider-web streets, hastening crowds, blinking signs, always the noise like a haze in the air. It looked new and hard and shiny. But then, he remembered, most of it was new, grown up in the last thirty years or less. Chance had grabbed an insignificant town on the slopes of the Cascades and made it the center of a continent.

He was glad that they landed outside the city proper, on a mountain shelf that overlooked it and bore a cluster of buildings which might have been erected only yesterday. Beyond them, lawns and gardens and tree-shaded lanes extended through a village of small homes. A high stone wall blocked off the end of a cliff that tumbled toward a misty gorge below. It was a nice place, he supposed.

The helicopter settled gently on a field, and Temple led Collie into a big building. It was, like most of them, a thing of curving lines and flat planes and enormous windows, faced with a smooth, pastel-tinted plastic. Within, it was quiet, a few people working at desks or going down the halls on errands. They stopped to stare at Collie and then, as if realizing the error, hurried on.

Temple took him into a dining hall where there were some others eating and ordered dinner for him. 'Just relax,' he said. 'We're all your friends here.'

'Ever'body eat in this place?' asked Collie.

'Not unless they want to. Most of them cook in their own houses, the same as anybody else. Just remember, all of us here are either like you or else here to help your kind. You're the real owner, or one of them.'

'I still ain't – I'm not sure just what you want of me.'

'To have you here, safe from danger. That's all, Collie. And don't be afraid, you won't be kept here longer than you yourself wish.'

'Hm.' Collie felt a little doubtful. Still, what the hell? He attacked the dinner with real appetite. It was good.

Afterward there was a session in a doctor's office, where they did a lot of incomprehensible things. 'It'll take about a week for complete examination,' said the doctor. 'We want to test everything we can. But right now you look good to me.'

Collie blushed, and was angry with himself for it.

'Just take it easy,' advised Temple as they left the building. 'Go take your tests at the laboratory, and the rest of the time you can do what you like. Get to know your neighbors. They'll show you the ropes. We have entertainment here every night – movies, dances, and so on. I think you'll enjoy yourself.'

Dusk was on them as they walked up the path toward the houses. Down at the foot of the road, the city opened a thousand eyes, glowed and winked and blazed like stars fallen to earth. Overhead, the sky was gentle with evening. Collie filled his lungs and let some of the tension ease out of him.

Gravel scrunched underfoot as they went by the lighted porches of the neat cottages. 'There are about a hundred living here right now,' said Temple. 'We've got places for five hundred before we have to build more. I hope we'll have to do that soon. But – I wonder . . . Here's yours, then. Here's your key. Go on, open it yourself, it's your house now.'

The interior was pleasantly and conveniently furnished. Temple moved unobtrusively about, showing Collie how to operate the gadgets. There were a lot of them. 'We'll send you some clothes in the morning, modern style,' he said. 'They'll be made up tonight according to your measurements. And here's some cash, in case you need it, and you can draw more whenever you wish.'

Collie's lips tightened. 'Look,' he said, 'I don't want charity.'

'You're not getting it. We need you worse than you need us. We're just grubstaking you.' Temple moved toward the door. 'I'll say goodnight now. Got work to do, may not see you for a while. If there's anything you want to know, or want help with, go ask the counsellor in the main office building. Good luck, Collie.'

When he was gone, there was an odd desolation. Collie felt very much alone. He wandered listlessly around the house, trying this and that. The color television was interesting, but it reminded him too much of the strangeness, little of it had any meaning for him. He sat down in a chair which molded itself to his body. 'Damn,' he muttered. 'Homesick already.'

4

The chiming at the door brought him to his feet. A look at the visiplate showed him a stranger outside. His hand dropped toward his knife, then he remembered it was in his bag – he'd have felt silly wearing it. 'Come in,' he said. His voice wobbled, and his anger at himself for that brought a return of steadiness, 'Come on in.'

He had never seen a negro before, though he recognized the type from descriptions – a tall young fellow, elegantly clad in an iridescent lounge suit. 'Hi, there.' The voice was deep and rich. 'Ah'm Joe Gammony.'

'Uh – Jim Collingwood.' They shook hands.

'Ah saw a new one was comin', an' mah wife an' me thought we'd ask you ovuh. Meet some o' the folks heah. Like to?'

'Why – sure. Thanks. Thanks a lot.' Collie remembered he had a supply cabinet. 'Like a drink first?'

'Sho', thanks, don' mind if Ah do.' Gammony accepted a glass and tossed it off with a grin. 'Hoo, boy! Goes down right, don' it?' He leaned easily against the wall, hands in pockets. 'Look, Jim, we-all is pretty free heah. Got to be. You don't mind a few questions, Ah hope?'

'N-no.'

'Well, Ah'll tell you 'bout mahself fuhst. Ah'm from Virginny, backwoods like Ah see you is. Been heah 'bout a year now. Ah was bo'n with a – kinesthesia, they call it. Got a perfec' sense o' balance an' direction. Nevah get lost. Walked when Ah was six months old, tha's why Ah got bowlegs.' He chuckled. 'Damn good pilot, too, when they'd taught me to fly. Don' need no instruments to tell me is Ah upside down or sideways to. Don' get dizzy easy, an' get ovuh it fast when Ah do. They're still findin' uses fo' mah sense. Tha's all.'

Collie told his own story and Gammony nodded without surprise. 'Tha's took a bigger chance than mine,' he said. 'Mine, it was jes' a little difference up in mah head somewheres, but you need a different bone an' muscle, some different at least, an' then they's yo' lungs, or mebbe it's yo' blood. They'll find that out. But Ah bet there ain't but one like you in the whole world. Come on, now, Jim – no, Collie, you said. Come on an' meet the folks.'

They went into the adjoining cottage. Gammony's wife was a pleasant negress, with a couple of children clinging wide-eyed to her skirts. 'The sprats ain't like me,' explained the father. 'Recessive mutation, Ah reckon, like most of 'em is.' He seemed to have learned a lot in a year, but then he seemed pretty bright too.

A small man with sharp dark eyes was introduced as Abe Feinberg, from Illinois. His hands were delicate, the extra joint in the thin fingers making them seem almost boneless. 'Highly developed tactile sense,' he said, 'together with ability to handle small things. It's useful for close work. I have a job finishing micrometric parts.'

Bulking over him, six and a half feet tall and so broad he seemed almost squat, was a blond giant. 'Misha Ivanovitch,' he said. 'Dey found me in Russia two years back – *da*, dey sheck a lot of de whole world. I'm just a strong man. Like a horse, strong.' He grinned. 'Not mosh use, dough. I'm not like a tractor strong.'

A slender, brown-haired girl, quite good-looking, said she was Lois Grenfell from Ontario. 'Unusual hearing – well into the super and subsonic ranges, with more tone discrimination than anyone else. Sure, of course I write music, but what's the use? Nobody else can hear the nuances.'

A gaunt, shock-haired man was paying her considerable attention. 'Tom O'Neill. They found me in Ireland. It's my eyes.

Telescopic vision. Oh, sure, I can see at ordinary distances too. There are several people I know of with straight telescopic, but they don't get in here. The poor divvils are having to wear glasses to see at less than a hundred feet.'

Alexander Arakelian of California, short and stout and dark, invited Collie to take a punch at him. 'Go ahead. Any time. Don't warn me.' Collie sprang, throwing his fist ahead, and nearly went to the floor as he missed. 'Sorry. Frankly, I didn't realize you'd be that fast. Damn near clipped me. Yeah, it's super-quick perception and reaction. Something about my nerve cells, they aren't sure just what.'

There were more. A good two dozen people were crowded into Gammony's living room. Collie couldn't remember all the names and traits. As he sat back with a glass in his hand, looking them over, he tried to think what it was they had in common.

First: They were all young. Obviously, none could be over twenty-eight, for the war had been twenty-nine years ago. The ages ranged from fifteen to the upper limit.

Second: They all looked pretty human. Any of them could pass for an ordinary, unmutated person unless you looked closely; the only odd one was a lightning calculator who happened to have eyes of brilliant red, not unpleasing. Feinberg, who seemed the most talkative man present, explained that a good mutation was, generally, something added to the normal human capacities. A man with boneless hands might be capable of highly delicate work, but he would be too specialized, not strong enough, to count as favorable. In like manner, there had been a lot of people born with both good and bad traits – a cripple with Miss Grenfell's type of hearing, for instance, or a superstrong moron. But they didn't count either.

Third: They were all well taken care of, highly paid, educated free for any work they chose. But the work seemed invariably to be such as they could do at home or in the shops and laboratories maintained up here.

Fourth: None of them were very happy.

It wasn't till later in the evening, when alcohol had dissolved most of his stiffness, that Collie really noticed this. It wasn't plain on them – it crept out in an occasional word, a sarcastic reference, a fleeting change of expression. He didn't know how to find out more about it. But hell and damnation, he had to know.

'Seems like they treat you pretty nice,' he ventured cautiously. He was sitting between Feinberg and Ivanovitch, on the fringes of the conversation.

'Yeah. I s'pose. I s'pose.' Feinberg had drunk a good deal, his cheeks were flushed and his voice not entirely under control. 'Lucky bastards. Born to the purple.'

'I been wonderin' what I could do. I'm just a farmer an' hunter.'

'They'll teach you. Hard to say, though. You and Misha are in pretty much the same boat. You can't do anything that a machine can't do better.'

Feinberg took out a cigaret and lit it and inhaled raggedly. 'That's the trouble with all of us, really. What the hell are we supposed to do? Sure, I get work sent up to me for finishing, and I do a good job on it, sure, sure. Only they could build a microfinisher to do it automatically. Keep Feinberg happy, though. Keep him too busy at his bench to think.'

'Nyet, it's not so bad,' said Ivanovitch heavily. 'I go roll rocks and swing a hammer, what's bad about dat? Better dan a liddle willage out in de woods and starving heff de time.'

'Oh, well, if you just want a full belly –' Feinberg looked glumly at his glass.

'Go on home, Collie,' he said all at once. 'Tell 'em to cram it. Go back where the deer and the antelope play, dig in the ground, hunt bears, raise a litter of kids. You'll be a lot more useful there than here.' He sensed Collie's hurt and laid a hand on his arm. 'It's for your own good, kid. I like you. I don't want to see you go through this damn mill.'

'What's the matter?' asked Collie. 'What's here you don't like?'

'Call it philosophical objections, if you want. Though there's a lot of practical ones. Talk to Joe Gammony, among others. He married a plain ordinary girl before they found him. Ask about the ways they tried to make him leave her behind when he came here. Ask about the way they've tried to get her from him ever since. Oh, no, nothing wicked. Nothing outright. No "or else" about it. We're all gentlemen here, we aren't vile Siberians. But they want to breed Joe to another of their superpeople. They don't want him wasting his genes on a mere human being.

'Some of us don't care. You been having you a hell of a good time, eh, Misha?' The giant grinned. Feinberg ran a hand through his own lank hair and went on. 'They introduced a girl to me. She lives up here too. Kinesthesia, like Joe's. They want her to have children by him, to reinforce the trait, and by me, to cross-breed. Throw in a lightning calculator and an Alaric Wayne brain, and you've got the super engineer, eh? Only Joe's a good Catholic, and I'm well, hell, I'm stubborn. I want to find my own dame and live a normal life.

'Normal! Hell, what's normal about this? What's normal about made work, a sop to keep you busy? What's normal about spending your life on a goddam mountaintop, always seeing the same people, always the same gossip. Sure, we're a pretty good bunch up here, in spite of our petty feuds and factions, but goddammit, there's a whole world outside. Hell, you don't even dare go downtown for a drink. You'd be lynched, Americans never did like privilege, unless they were the ones who had it. I don't even like it when it's mine. My people were kicked around too long for me to subscribe to any Master Race.

'Just ask yourself, Collie. Ask yourself what *is* a superman. What *is* a favorable mutation? What real basis did they have for choosing us? What good are we?

'What good is the whole mucking program? Hell, we're all full of mutated genes. Every living thing on Earth is. We're not going to lick the problem by trying to breed supermen. The supermen are just as likely to beget crippled idiots as anyone else.

'They say Nietzsche preached the superman. That only proves they never bothered to read Nietzsche. This is not what he had in mind. Shaw, there was the real superman-monger. Sure, he was clever, witty, humane, but he couldn't *think*. He lacked depth. Down underneath, he despised the scientific method. So do most of us. Maybe rightly so, because it's inhuman. It's inhuman to look at the world so coldly. People aren't reasonable. It's much more comfortable to look around for a father image – and hell, if you can't find one, you make one. You breed him!'

Collie went home about midnight. He felt tired, drained of strength with all he had seen and heard this day. The world could not be the same for him, not ever again, and he wished most desperately that it could. But it was long before he got to sleep.

5

The counsellor said, 'Frankly, I can't think of any job for you which would use your special abilities. But you have a good intelligence, so there's no reason why you couldn't go into something like engineering.'

'Well –' Collie scratched his head. 'I heard talk 'bout sponge divin', off Florida. I can hold my breath good, you know.'

'That's just to supply a backward local market,' said the counsellor gently. 'Our sponges are synthetic. I'm afraid there wouldn't be any place for you in the trade.'

'It was just a thought. I could do a lot better with your scoutin' teams among the backwoods people.'

'Sorry, we couldn't permit that. It would be dangerous for you.'

Collie bristled. 'Look here. I'm a free citizen an' I can go where I damn well want.'

'We can't stop you from leaving,' said the counsellor, 'but we can refuse you a job.' He smiled. 'Let's not argue about this. It's for your own good. We want you to be safe and prosperous, that's all.'

'Well –' Collie backed down. He wasn't used to arguing. Among his folk, you kept your voice low or you stepped outside – nothing in between. 'Well, mebbe you're right. I'll have to think about it.'

'Take all the time you want,' said the counsellor. 'But wouldn't you like to go to school? We'll be starting a new class, three hours a day, very soon.'

'Yeah – yeah, I reckon so. Thanks.' Collie got out as quickly as he could.

He slouched gloomily along the walk toward his house. Goddammit all, anyway. Abe Feinberg might be right, at that. Only what could you do? Go back home – after all his brave excited words? It didn't appeal to him. Even if he announced his intention of doing so, they'd argue and stall and make excuses. They'd find ways to make retreat just too embarrassing for him. He swung clenched fists at his sides. This was like being meshed in cobwebs. Fine and silky and gluey.

As he stamped onto his porch, he noticed Misha Ivanovitch passing by. The big Russian was whistling cheerfully to himself. 'Hey,' called Collie, 'how 'bout a drink with me?'

'*Da.*' Ivanovitch grinned and turned around. 'I hev trobble saying no in American.'

They entered the cottage, leaving the door open to the summer air. Collie sloshed whiskey into two glasses. 'I'm gettin' tired o' drinkin' up here,' he said after the third round. 'I never even been downtown.'

'I hev,' said Ivanovitch. 'Dey got bars and t'ings.'

'Let's go!'

'Well –' Ivanovitch's big mild face clouded. 'We ain't so very welcome down dere.'

'Goddammit, we're free people, ain't we?' Collie stalked toward the door. 'If you don't want to go, I'll go alone.'

'Hokay. I'll kip you out of trobble, mebbe.'

The sun was low as they walked rapidly down the path. Collie wanted to run, he could have been at his goal in minutes, but Ivanovitch's lumbering gait would have been left behind. As they descended, the city was no longer a neat relief map, it rose and spread until they were between houses. Here cars sped past, purring ovoids that flashed with metal and plastic, and there were more people around than Collie was used to. The liquor was dying in him, and he wondered if he might not have been foolish, but too late now. He'd look a proper fool turning back, wouldn't he?

'We get dat bus, huh?' Ivanovitch stepped out on a curb.

The long gray vehicle stopped for them, and they boarded it and found seats. Collie craned his neck to look around. About twenty passengers, they all seemed very ordinary city folk. There were a couple of mutants, of course – a young man with a lumpy, almost canine face, and another quite hairless. Not for the first time, Collie wanted to thank God for his own genes. *If I'd been like that* –

But what was this mysterious 'I' which reached back a few years and forward an unknown number of days? What was it that housed in his skull and looked out at the world, forever a prisoner within itself, and – and – Collie drew back from the thought with a shudder.

During his reverie, the bus had reached the loop. 'Let's get off here,' said Ivanovitch. 'I know a place.' Collie envied the giant's placidity as they paid and debarked. Then his feelings were lost in sheer wonder.

The buildings around him were not extremely high – thirty stories was the limit, for the city had been planned as decentralized to reduce the traffic problem. But to him they were mountainous, sheer walls looming overhead, tier upon tier of frozen waterfalls, dizzying spires, flashing glass, signs winking and glaring through the young twilight. The city roared around him, hurrying faceless crowds, rainbow of garments, clattering shoes on hard pavement, a steady, restless grumble of traffic, voices and voices and voices. He shrank close to Ivanovitch and let himself be led.

They entered a tavern. It was a long dim-lit room, booths on one side and the bar on the other. 'Live' murals moved sensuously on the walls, and the television was flickering in one corner. The place was pretty full, men coming off work and stopping in for a drink, and the talking and laughing was like a storm in his skull.

Ivanovitch bellied up to the bar, easing others aside, and thumped it so the glasses jumped. 'Two vodkas,' he said. 'Beer chasers.'

Collie sipped the liquid fire cautiously and looked around him with large eyes. At first glance, there was an incredible gaiety here, like a festival at home. Then you looked closer and saw the worn faces and the weary eyes, and you heard the voices more clearly. He wondered if anyone in here was really happy.

But why should that be? These people had more to eat and wear and see and do then he had ever known; they had comfortable houses, no need to carry weapons, medicine like witchcraft to ease their hurts. Collie had no illusions about the 'natural life.' It was toil and endurance, rain and snow and harrying wind, hunger and sickness and early death. What was it that lay like a worm in these men and women?

Someone tapped his shoulder. He looked around to see a burly, middle-aged man, roughly clad, weaving a bit on his feet. His face was red and his lip stuck out belligerently. 'You with that guy?' he asked, jerking a finger at Ivanovitch's broad back.

'Well – yes.' Collie felt a tightness in his stomach.

'From up on the hill, huh?'

Collie remembered warnings he'd had, but it was too late now. 'Yeah,' he said. 'We, uh, we wanted to, well, come down an' make friends.'

'*Friends!*' The drunk lifted his hands. 'When'd the boss ever make friends with the hired help? I work all day, go home too mucking tired to think, and they take my money for taxes and spend it on you!'

Ivanovitch turned around, narrowing his eyes. 'We ain't looking for trobble,' he said.

'Nah. I'll bet you're not. Why should you? You got all you want already. Live like kings. Now you're coming down here slumming. Want to throw us a bone, huh, after we kept you so long?'

'*From up on the hill . . . Supermen . . . Too good for us . . .*' There were others now, closing in, a ring of hard faces and angry eyes. Collie tautened, feeling himself tremble.

The bartender leaned over. 'Look, you fellows better get out. I don't want no trouble.'

Ivanovitch growled, deep in his throat. 'We got just as mosh right in here as you,' he muttered.

'As much right!' The drunk who had spoken first laughed unpleasantly. 'Yeah. I'll say you do!'

'My kids ain't up on the hill,' said someone else. 'They ain't good enough, like this here furriner.'

'I'm not either.' A mutant shook his hair-covered face. 'They can't use me. I'm only good enough to pay these bastards' keep.'

'Come on,' whispered Collie. He plucked urgently at Ivanovitch's sleeve. 'Come on, Misha, let's leave.'

'Hokay, we go,' said the Russian sourly. He reached out a brawny arm and shoved three men aside. That was when the riot started.

Collie felt something explode in his face. A fist! He struck back, wildly. The crowd yelled and pressed in.

Ivanovitch roared. He knocked two heads together and tossed the victims into the mob. Hands battered at him, ripping his clothes. He surged forward, slapping. Heads rocked on their necks.

Collie braced himself, back to the bar. As the men shoved in against him, he pushed with his feet. Two of them lurched from him. The crowd pushed them back. He slugged hard, into the nearest face. A fist in his belly knocked the wind from him. He sagged, gasping, and they kicked at his ankles. Gulping back air, he crouched low and started to fight.

'Back to back!' whooped Ivanovitch. He spread his legs far apart and glared at the mob. Three lay unconscious before him. The rest moved aside, snarling.

A siren howled. Blue uniforms filled the doorway, and nightsticks prodded a way through the turmoil. 'Awright, awright! Break it up there!'

Collie stood breathing hard. Through the window he saw a neon sign across the street, flashing and flashing, insane gibberish of light. He retched. It was not a hurt, it was the sick loneliness that rose in him. They hated him. The world roared and stamped and whirled, grinding, eating, hating, and he wanted to run until he was home again. He wanted to cry.

'You're all under arrest here,' shouted one of the policemen. 'You're all going down to the station. Now quiet down!'

As they left the bar, Collie saw an automobile drawn up across the way, and a man and a dog standing on its hood and looking over the gathered crowd. It was only a glimpse, and he didn't think much of it then. The man was a slim young fellow, well-dressed, ordinary looking in his coat and hat. It was the dog that Collie noticed now – a big ungainly creature, shaggy and dark, with too large a head. A mutant dog.

6

The capitol stood in its own parks and gardens near the center of town. It was a tall building of many columned tiers, rising to a high spire from which fluttered the banner of the North American Union. Above the first-floor colonnade, a dove in relief spread its wings over the globe of Earth. To the irreverent, building, flag, and symbol were the Steeple, the Jack and Stripes, and the Pigeon; to Alaric Wayne they were wistfulness.

He came up the long flight of stairs, and the guards saluted and let him and the dog pass without challenge. Down a marbled corridor to an automatic elevator, and then up toward the tenth-floor conference room. Alaric Wayne fumbled out a cigaret and lit it and puffed in nervous jerks. Always there was this tightening inside him, the fear of meeting the men whom he dominated. What words would they understand? He sighed, and reached down to ruffle the dog's misshapen head. The wish to be liked, to be accepted as an anonymous member of the group, was strong within him. He recognized it and fought it down, but he could never get rid of it. Because what psychiatrist could help a brain unlike anything ever seen on Earth before?

Another guard outside the chamber snapped to attention as he approached. He winced, inwardly, and passed by with a nod. He was not much to look at, this young man with strangeness inside his skull: medium height, slender-boned awkward body, thin straight features and large light eyes under rumpled brown hair. The suit and coat disguised his short body and long legs and big head. They were not so different from the human as to be a deformity, or even very noticeable, but he felt his shape as another mark on him.

The door opened automatically, and he walked into the long, quiet room. At its farther end, the wall was clear plastic, overlooking the city and the mountains and the nightfall. There were half a dozen men gathered around the table, waiting for him. They were all human, being in their forties, fifties, and sixties, and they ruled the continent, but they had been waiting for him.

Robert Boyd, President of North America, turned a weary face toward Wayne as he entered. 'Hello, Alaric,' he said. His voice was toneless, flat and discouraged. The others nodded and murmured greetings: Nason, the chief of staff; Ramorez, majority leader in Congress; Winkelreid, minister of foreign affairs; de Guise, minister of health and genetics; Cunningham, McKenna, Giovanni, assistants.

Wayne paused. His lips opened, but for a moment no words would come out, a sudden wall in his head. 'I – I – I –' He closed his mouth and tried again. They waited, patient with his speech impediment. 'Sorry I'm late. There was a riot downtown and I s-stayed to watch because w-w-w-one of your hill dwellers was involved.'

'Eh?' De Guise leaned forward, his voice sharpening. 'Which one? What trouble?'

'That big Russian, what's his name, Ivanovitch. Bar, nullbad, arre – Sorry!' Wayne snapped his thin fingers in annoyance. Damn it, wouldn't he ever get used to ordinary speech? Even if his mind didn't work the way theirs did, he ought to be able to talk intelligibly. He paused, sorting the one thread out of the web of his thoughts. 'No one seemed badly hurt. The police were arresting everybody. It was in a bar downtown.'

De Guise smiled without much humor. 'I'll let him wait till morning before having him bailed out. The big ox! He should know better by now than to mingle with townspeople.'

'It's not so good,' said Ramorez. 'I've told you again and again, all of you, it can't go on. You can't segregate a special class, give it special privileges, and expect to fit it into a democratic society.'

'We'll have to, that's all,' shrugged Boyd.

'If necessary, we can change the society,' said Nason. 'The human race as a whole is more important than a particular form of government.'

'I'm not so sure of that,' said Ramorez.

'Hell, man,' snorted Nason, 'if there isn't a human race, there won't be a government of any kind.'

'We've been through all this before,' said Boyd. 'There's another item on the agenda today. Unless –' He looked at Wayne, who had seated himself.

The mutant shook his head, smiling faintly. 'Sorry. I've tried to work out an ideal political solution for you, but human beings aren't my forte. I think too differently. Much easier to work with electrons and potential fields, I assure you.'

'Which may be why the world blew up in our faces, thirty years ago,' said Boyd. 'And why it's getting set to blow up again.'

Wayne looked at him with a surprised blankness. It was a curiously innocent look, like a child's. 'It's that bad?' he asked. 'I haven't heard the news in a long time.'

No, thought Boyd, *you've immured yourself in that incredible nest up on the Continental Divide, you've locked yourself away like a sorcerer from a world that doesn't understand you. Now and then you come down from Sinai with something for us – the atomic motor, the power-transmitting beam, the complete mathematical theory of turbulence, oh, a hundred things that are going to transform our whole civilization. But why do you do it? What have you got in common with us?*

He spoke slowly: 'Well, it isn't an acute crisis – yet. It may not be for a long time. The Siberian government is too canny for that. But they plan a long way ahead – their eugenics program is only one case of that – and we know they're working against us.' He gestured to the map which hung on one wall, below the lined, moody face of the late great President Drummond. 'The geopolitical facts of life haven't changed. Anyone who can unite the Eurasia-African heartland against us will turn the Americas into an outlying island which can be gobbled up at leisure. And Siberia is working toward that aim.'

'Why, we've got our bases on the moon, haven't we?' asked Wayne. The surprised look was still on him. 'We can bombard them from s-s-s-space.'

'They've got bases up there too, don't forget.'

'They have?'

'You didn't *know*?' Boyd pulled his jaw up again. 'Yes, they do. We were too weak to prevent their establishing them, fifteen years ago. The two sets of bases simply cancel: in case of war, they'll wreck each other. Unless you can think up something.'

'Well,' said Wayne, 'there might be possibilities of making a force-screen. I'll have to think about it.'

They accepted the statement casually, all but Nason, who muttered a delighted oath. They had come to expect the impossible from Wayne – the impossibly good and the impossibly bad.

'You know,' said Nason after a while, 'I'm not too happy about your staying alone up in the mountains, Al. Even if you do have defenses, still, I wish you'd at least permit me to send up a guard.'

Wayne looked down at his hands. He didn't answer, he couldn't bring himself to do so, but they knew it was a refusal.

De Guise thrust out an aggressive chin. 'For that matter, if you'll excuse a well-worn and personal subject, you ought to be on the hill, in my colony. At the very least, you ought to be having children, or giving us a gamete deposit. Your chromosomes are unique. You can't let them die with you.'

Wayne flushed, and the dog growled, ever so faintly. He tried to answer this time. 'N-n-n-n – *No!*' It came out shrilly.

De Guise relapsed. 'I'm sorry,' he mumbled.

'What we asked you to come here about,' said Boyd hastily, 'was this Mars expedition.'

'Mars – Oh, yes. That. You got my designs for the spaceship, didn't you?'

'The complete report. Of course. But why do you want us to go to Mars? You forgot to mention that fact.'

Wayne blinked. 'Isn't it obvious?' he replied. 'It's the answer to your problem of mutation. The radiation is still around. It will be for decades yet. It will keep on distorting genes, making heredity ever more unpredictable.' He was speaking fast now, without hesitation. The subject was the kind he liked, big and complex and wholly impersonal. 'Before the war, it wasn't thought that much mutation would be produced by atomic indiscretions. The level of resistance to change seemed high among mammals, judging by experiments. It seemed obvious that an amount of change such as has actually occurred could not happen without a radiation intensity which would kill off all life anyway.

'But they didn't foresee the *pervasiveness* of it. Dust particles, irradiated air molecules, irradiated atoms in the food we eat and the water we drink – radiation everywhere. The intensity was not high enough to do serious damage to most organisms, but it was everywhere, in *all* the body, between the cells, in the protoplasm itself. So naturally the nucleoproteins in the genes went crazy.'

Boyd lifted his hand, trying to stem the rush, but Wayne's eyes were bright and blank, not noticing him, the strange mind had gone off into its own world again. Boyd sat back with a sigh, preparing himself for a lecture on the obvious. That was Wayne's style of talk – starting from the elements and covering everything. At that, this speech was fairly coherent; sometimes he wove in and out between topics so that nobody could unscramble what he said.

'Now of course we're working on techniques of direct observation and manipulation of genes. We've got to have them, and I think eventually we will. But it may take a long time, generations perhaps. There are some tremendous difficulties in the way: the Heisenberg Uncertainty Principle is one of them, setting a theoretical limit which, somehow, we *must* get around. Meanwhile, life on Earth is choked with distorted genes. Only a fraction of them can have appeared overtly as yet, in spite of the enormous incidence of mutants.

'I predict a sharp decline of the birth rate within the next few years, a decline which will accelerate as more and more lethal or sterilizing recessives chance to find their mates. And moreover, Earth's whole ecology, which supports all life including man, is going to go out of kilter as its delicate balance is upset. Just try living if nitrogen-fixing bacteria, to give one example, become extinct! All higher forms of life may disappear if the situation isn't remedied by man; and as yet, we don't know how to remedy it.

'Things are already bad; but the radiation is still there, with lessened intensity but strong enough to make matters worse. No *type* is stable. Not even mutants will breed true. How can we even study genetics under such conditions? And if the problem of heredity-control takes a hundred years to solve, there may be nobody left to use the solution.

'Attempts have been made to build sealed-off laboratories. They haven't worked well – there is just too much radioactivity around. The background count is too high for precision work, no matter how much you seal and purify and decontaminate.

Moreover, many specimens, I mean *many* at a time, will be needed for thorough study. You can't build a sealed chamber big enough to hold them.

'It has been proposed to set up colonies on Luna. The idea is sound in principle, but in practice it has flaws. It would be too difficult to make the moon self-supporting, and too expensive to support it from Earth. Then, too, I gather that there are hostile bases on the moon, which could make trouble.

'But no one has yet gone beyond the Earth-Luna system. I propose to do so. Venus, we know by astronomy, is a hellish place, even worse than Luna. Mars is not too hospitable, either, but it has possibilities. There is oxygen enough for an efficient compressor to keep men alive. There is a little water – probably a good deal locked up in minerals. There must be heavy metals in fair abundance which are scarce on the moon. There is life of some sort, we know, which would furnish invaluable subjects and controls for the genetic studies, as well as, possibly, food. The cold is not a great problem when we have atomic energy. The rocket fuel required to get there is not much more than that required for Luna. And there is plenty of surface area. I am convinced that self-supporting colonies could be established there.

'By this we would gain – well, first, suitable laboratory conditions. Second, the colonists would no longer be mutating, and if the research fails would have a better prospect of survival than life on Earth. Third, they would be a select group, which would accomplish your purpose of eugenics without the friction involved in your present segregation policy. A policy which looks as if it will break down soon anyway.'

Wayne stopped. De Guise nodded gloomily. 'I know it is,' he said. 'If the hill dwellers aren't mobbed first, they'll leave in disgust. But what else could we do, I ask you?'

'Hm – Mars.' Winkelreid looked out the window at the darkening sky. 'Yes. I have information that the Siberians are thinking along similar lines. Perhaps we had better get to work on your ship.'

Cunningham cleared his throat. 'My engineers have looked at your plans already,' he said, 'and have several objections to make.

The instruments and controls –'

'I know,' said Wayne. 'It's all right. I appreciated the need for haste, and so designed a very simplified ship. The crew will be able to take over the functions of many things you would ordinarily leave to machines.'

'The crew?'

'Your supermen, of course. The hill dwellers. And I will be the captain.'

That brought the storm down on Wayne.

Boyd sat on the edge of the quarrel, taking no part in it. He knew who was going to win. His eyes strayed out to the window and the early night and the thousand twinkling lights of homes. On such summer evenings, once during a long-buried year, he had been wont to sit in the Café Flores, watching life go by. There would be an aperitif in his hand, which was not to be drunk but to be savored, as part of the dusk and the city and the thousand human faces passing. There had been a little Finnish girl studying in the same classes as he, they'd seen a lot of each other, for they were young and this was Paris and all the world lay before them.

It was funny how often he thought of that year. And the Winged Victory. He liked to go to the Louvre when it was open at night. You came up a long flight of stairs, and there she was at the head of them, limned against darkness, straining into the wind, and you could see the surge frozen in her, hear the streaming wind and the wild blowing of trumpets and the great thunder of wings. It would be a sea wind, he thought. It couldn't be anything else flowing and crying around that striding triumph.

Ashes to ashes, dust to dust. I am the Resurrection and the Life, saith the Lord. But there was no more Finnish girl, no more Paris, no more Nike of Samothrace. There was night.

7

PRIDE: Alaric: the conqueror; Wayne: wain, wagon, traveling and wandering into unknownness. Thus: the wain which will carry the conqueror beyond the sky. The hollow conqueror.

Emptiness within. Loneliness forever. But no more weeping alone in darkness since the night the rocket crashed and bore in flames

	(	Father	)	
	(		)	
Roderick Wayne	:	God	:	
	(		)	
	(	Shield	)	
				– Belongingness,
	(	Mother	)	
	(		)	
Karen Wayne	:	Beloved	:	
	(		)	
	(	Home	)	

for on that night all the the tears were used up and there are no more.

Fifth of his line, Grouchy the dog tries to help and understand. But there is so little he can do. There is not full communication (basic function of man-as-man, to differentiate him from man-as-animal), there can only be the absence of fear.

The conqueror fears, alone within himself. He does not think these other two-legs wish him ill. But he does not understand, and they do not understand, and he must fight to talk in their words.

Self-pity: a worm feeding on his own tail. Enough. They are building the motors now.

Energy of escape: and beautiful is the matrix that no one else knows.

Leaves are bronze and gold and flying red flame. The wind from the darkening pole is cold on cheeks and hands.

'Mr. Wayne?'

'Yes –' (His name? They told you once. Oh, yes.) 'What is it, Mr. Collingwood?'

'I been thinkin'. I think I'd like to be in your crew after all.'

'Thank you. I am glad of that.'

'I, uh, well, at first it seemed kind of a wild notion. I was all set to go home. But then I figgered this was a chance to do something real useful.' Glow of eyes: 'An' it ought to be fun, too!'

'Well, you'll be an engineering assistant on the voyage. It w-w-wouldn't hurt if y-y-y-you –'

'Studied? Oh, sure, Mr. Wayne. I'm doin' that. I'll be all set by springtime. Only one thing I been wonderin' about. Why leave then? Ain – isn't Mars closer later in the year?'

'To be sure. However, the plan is to swing close around the sun and do a certain amount of the blasting in that neighborhood. It will save time and reaction mass, since we will be utilizing the gravitational potential energy of the mass with respect to the sun, and – well, it has all been worked out.'

All of it. A thick volume of calculations, tables, curves, for the benefit of the men who will stay behind. It is all contained in one Wayne matrix equation.

But they don't think that way. They have to take one thing at a time, step by step. The huge network of simultaneously interacting factors, the enormous unity of it, that is meaningless to them, they have to crawl link by link through its mesh and the entire picture is never really there.

But they see what you cannot. You must have most of the totality before you can consider it at all – anything less is an ungraspable fragment, jagged in infinity. They can seize that one piece, and hold it to them, and make it their own. Unrelatedness does not fill them with a blind unconscious panic, so that their minds recoil from it and thinking blurs.

Practicality: A web of equations, diagrams, and shining metal. Potential fields, mathematical abstractions more real, somehow, than the wind and the earth and the far pale sun.

Practicality: There will be one woman along. We need her

106

hearing. She can pick out subsonics and supersonics, analyze them, tell us as surely as any instrument

> which would have to be painstakingly designed and built and tested and re-designed and rebuilt (consuming time, and time gallops like a wild horse)

> which would have to include a massive computer (but the human brain, a couple of pounds of wet spongy tissue, can do the same work if you train it properly)

> which would have to . . . (equations again, a vague adumbration – no! Too much else to think about)

how the rockets are functioning. Still: I wish there could be some other way. One unmarried woman, a little on the prim side, and seven men – why don't human beings behave as sensibly as electrons?

The conqueror is too afraid of women to know them. He could have almost any one he asked for, but there would be too much strangeness in her eyes. What would she be thinking, alone within herself?

Snow is chill and glittering, blue shadows under a high thin heaven. 'Hello, Mr. Feinberg. How's it going?'

'Just fine, Mr. Wayne, just fine. I'd never appreciated how much work had to go into a spaceship. Every plate in her hull is a chunk of precision equipment, huh? But we're getting her built, and we'll nurse her to Mars all right.' Glow: 'God, you don't know what this means to me! I was going to go home. I was spending my life fiddling around with stuff that didn't mean a thing. Now I can work on this.'

Curious, the romance in cold steel and bare equations. We have to set up a special office just to turn away would-be crewmen. But when she finally stands on her tail and blows flame and thunder, that will be a high and proud moment.

Captain Wayne, pilot officers O'Neill, Arakelian, and Gammony, engineers Feinberg, Collingwood, and Grenfell, general crewman Ivanovitch, their names will be bright in history. But they would go even if it were not to be recorded at all. In the months of training and indoctrination, they are shaking down into a team. Even the dog Grouchy is accepted to a degree. There is no obvious reason to carry his mass and appetite along, but

Captain Wayne desires it.

(Companionship. The habit of thinking out loud, talking incomprehensibly to a dog with too much brain. Perhaps the dog even understands some of it. We would be very lost without each other, but we need not tell them that. Let Grouchy go as mascot.)

Rivers brawl noisily between crumbling snowbanks, earthdark puddles ruffle and stir under a bright cold wind, the sky is becoming clangorous with returning birds. 'Oh, she tested wonderfully. I don't think she'll give much trouble. You might overhaul that No. Three timer, though, just for luck.'

'Excellent, Mr. Arakelian. We'll soon be on our way.'

' "It's Johnny Bowlegs, pack your kit and trek." Okay, fine, Mr. Wayne.'

I would like to call them by their first names. But somehow I cannot do it. I cannot know exactly what they would think of it. And as long as I remain formal, so will they. Well, there is safety in formality. It is a good mask.

The first tender green, as if spring had just breathed on the bare dark limbs. 'Well, Al, tomorrow's the big day.'

'Tomorrow midnight, yes.'

'If you aren't back inside a year, we'll come looking for you.' How often has President Boyd said that?

'No need. Give us a few months extra. I can always calculate an orbit on short notice, if we get off schedule.'

'You know, sometimes I think you want to stay there.'

'Well, Mars has i-i-its points.'

The lights glare out of darkness. The ship is a hundred-foot pillar reaching up toward the invisible stars. Machines grind and rumble through the humming, chattering voices. A sweep-second hand goes quickly around, once, twice, three times, four times, the minute hand crawls toward midnight. But this is now. We must always live in now. It is a crippling thing to the network mind. But that mind has been lamed by growing up in strangeness, it will always limp and fumble. 'I needn't wish you good luck. You know what we think of you people.'

The doors hiss softly shut. The atomics thutter, warming up the firing chamber. A relay clicks. Metal enfolds like a colder womb. 'Testing one, two, three. Testing one, two, three.'

Mesh of energies, the potential fields forming oneness, continuum around the curve of the universe. Consider the equations of an interplanetary orbit. Space and time are relational concepts only. The energy-relation of the ship to sun-Earth-Mars-universe is going to be changed.

'Number One bank ready.'

'Number Two bank ready.'

'Number Three bank ready.'

'Stand by. All hands stand by . . . or lie by, as the case may be. Four seconds to go, three, two.'

Easy. Grouchy, easy, lie there and let the giant's hand stuff you back into your couch. Lie there and wait.

'Fire!'

Roar and rumble and shriek, pressure, darkness ragged before the eyes, outward bound.

Energy requirement equals the integral of the gravitational function from Earth-surface to infinity.

8

Beyond the viewports there was night and the stars, flash and glitter and cold blackness to the end of forever. Collie turned from the sight with a shiver along his nerves. Sometimes, on winter nights in the mountains, he had seen the sky almost as chill and pitilessly brilliant, but never just like this. Never from a shell of metal and plastic and thrumming force, unrestful between the worlds. Here Earth was a double star, amber and blue, high mountains and windy plains and the great tramping seas were shrunk to a fleck of light.

The rockets droned and shivered, always talking, always in his flesh. Collie slept with that voice in him, here as they rounded the sun, weaving in and out of uneasy dreams, growling and sighing and mumbling of loneliness. It was no place for a man.

He grew aware that Lois Grenfell was standing beside him there in the narrow, girder-barred passage between living quarters and engine room. Her wide eyes were looking past him, out at the stars, but there was a blankness to tell she did not really see them.

'Hi,' he said awkwardly.

''Lo.' She turned to face him. 'How're you?'

Idle question, when you lived and breathed, washed and ate and worked and slept together, day after day, no more privacy than two cells in the same body. Quarrels had begun when they were hardly a week out from Earth, though nothing had become serious yet. Collie had tended to withdraw into his own shyness, saying little to anyone.

'Okay, I reckon,' he told her. With an attempt to smile: 'You got nothin' to complain of, neither. One gal with seven men.'

'It isn't easy,' she said, 'and it's going to get harder. I may have made a mistake, coming along.'

'Captain Wayne, he'd'a known if –'

'Wayne!' Suddenly she flared at him, with rawness in her voice. 'Always Wayne, Wayne the infallible, Wayne the invincible, Wayne the superman. Why can't people see that he's blind? Why can't they see that he knows less about human beings than a backwoods trapper? He just threw together such of us as would fit into his machine – he never thought we might be more than cogs.'

Collie lifted his hand, as if to fend her off. He felt shocked by the blaze in her. 'Take it easy,' he murmured. 'Take it easy, Lois.'

She subsided, leaning against the wall and looking at the floor. 'I'm sorry.'

'Mebbe you should rest a bit. You look tired.'

'I can't rest. There's too much noise.'

'Yeah – yeah, it's pretty loud for you, isn't it?'

'Not that,' she said. 'I can get used to the volume of it, the same as you. But to you it's just background, unchanging, like the hull itself. I can always hear the changes. A little flutter here, a shifting tone there, a creaking and a whispering – and I sit up wondering what it means, wondering if something's about to give and if we aren't going to go spinning away till the end of time. It's never the same! I can't ever get used to it!'

'I see,' he said. 'I see.'

'Then there's Tom. He – well – you know. And I like him a lot, but – And I know sooner or later Misha's going to make a pass at me, he can't help himself, and there'll be trouble. And the others, how long will they stay the way they are? I don't know, and I get scared.'

Her hands were grasping at his, blindly in search of comfort, and he took them without thinking. 'Once we reach Mars, things'll get better,' he said.

'Why did you come along?' she asked slowly.

'I dunno,' he said. 'Same reason as the rest, I suppose. This seemed like a big an' worthwhile thing to do. But out here, you get to wonderin' if anything we can do matters very much.'

'I like you, Collie,' she said impulsively. 'There's something about you, I don't know what . . . yes, maybe I do. All the rest of us, everyone else aboard this ship, we're all twisted up, frustrated one way or another, full of doubt and weakness. You grew up in a cleaner world.'

His face was hot. 'I get scared too,' he mumbled, looking away.

'It's a healthy fright, then. You –'

A footstep on the companionway from the bridge: Collie turned to look into O'Neill's gaunt face. He had a brief wish to jerk his hands back from Lois – she wasn't his girl – but he thrust it down. 'Hi, Tom,' he said.

The Irishman's mouth grew crooked. 'Hello,' he said. Then, very quietly: 'You too, eh?'

'Me too, what?' Collie hedged.

O'Neill sighed. 'Never mind. I don't like scenes.'

Lois gave him a cold look. 'For your information,' she said, 'I was talking to Collie because he's the only one I can talk to without worrying over what he really means.'

'And Joe Gammony, perhaps – or the dog.' O'Neill chuckled, a sad little sound under the pulsing of the rockets. 'Well, no matter, I was looking for both of you on business. The Old Man doesn't quite like something about the engines. He says he can't put his finger on the trouble, but he's sure something is amiss.'

'The instruments read pretty good,' said Collie. "Course, with new-type engines like this, you can't never tell, but –' His voice trailed off, and there was a sudden lump of chill in him.

'I –' Lois' face drew into a frown, and her eyes clouded. 'I can't be sure, Tom. There's been a sort of new pattern lately in the noise. A supersonic buzz from the tubes themselves, that hasn't been there before. I don't know what it means. I listened to this thing on the test stand and the test flights till I thought I'd memorized every noise it could make. But lately –'

'No one,' said O'Neill softly, 'has ever taken a spaceship this far before now.'

Collie spoke through a stiffness in his throat. 'I know how our orbit's laid out. If the engines quit on us at this time, an' we don't get them workin' again mighty fast, we'll be too close to the sun to pull away. We'll prob'ly fall into the sun.'

They stood unmoving while the metal sang around them, thinking of that fire-sheathed immensity they had watched through shielded ports.

'Wayne's mind can analyze the sounds he can hear, and the instrument readings he can see, and get a pattern out of them,' said O'Neill at last, grimly. 'But he can only hear divvil a few of 'em; he hasn't got enough data. You can hear it all, macushla, but you can't fit it into a complete picture the way he can.'

She looked at Collie with a certain weariness. 'I told you,' she said in a flat voice. 'I told you Wayne thought of us as cogs in a machine, and we aren't.'

'Well,' said O'Neill, 'the skipper wants you to write down what you can hear, Lois. You know, on that multisonic scale they worked out for you. And Collie, will you be talking to Abe about this?'

The hillman nodded and left, moving along the rat-hole passageway toward the rear bulkhead.

Beyond it was a narrow engine-control room, the rear wall a single gleaming constellation of instruments and switches and dials. Abe Feinberg looked up from his seat. 'What are you doing?' he asked. 'You don't go on duty for three hours yet.'

Collie explained. Feinberg scowled. 'I don't like that new flutter in the ion-blast meters,' he said. 'But the potential fields seem to be holding fairly steady.'

He opened a drawer and took out the diagrams of the ship. Collie had pored over them till his eyes swam, and now he followed their intricacies without much trouble. Beyond the heavily shielded room in which he stood was the water-jacketed pile that was their energy source; water fed in automatically from the surrounding storage space to the pile chamber, where it was converted to superheated steam which was then electrically torn apart. The ions, positive and negative, were fed out through their various tubes, their course regulated by potential fields; in effect, each tube was a huge-scale linear accelerator. It was, in principle, a simple arrangement; but the multitude of control systems, interwoven and feeding back into each other, made it hard for anyone but Wayne to understand as a totality.

'Hm.' Feinberg shook his head. 'I dunno. There's a flutter in the blast, all right, and it's building up; but what's causing it? And what'll it lead to?'

'It'd be a funny way to die,' murmured Collie. 'A bit o' the sun, shinin' forever in the sky. It could be worse.' He grinned without much humor. 'Not that I want to, you understand.'

Feinberg gave him a sharp look. 'Don't let it get you, Collie,' he said at last. 'This that's around us is bigger than anything man was ever meant for, but we'll just have to remember we're human. We'll just have to keep going, and not think too much.'

Collie held his breath, listening to the *broom-broom-broom* of the rockets and the many whispers and creakings and mutterings that wove around it. Was it only his imagination, or could he hear a saw-edged whine in that noise? And if he could, did it mean anything?

Eight mutant humans, knit so closely together with their ship that it could hardly stir without all of them, riding a fireball no man had ever really tested into a sky no man had ever seen – For the first time, it shocked home to him what a long chance Alaric Wayne was taking. What a wild and reckless stunt this voyage was. He must have dominated the rulers of America like a god to make them agree to this.

Sure, sure, the mission was of terrible urgency, but even so! For an instant Collie felt a rage in him at the silent man who had thus carelessly thrown them out beyond heaven. Didn't the crazy bastard care what happened, even to himself?

Slowly, then, Collie began to see that Wayne didn't care. Not very much.

It explained a lot of things, but it left him feeling cold.

An hour slipped by, and another. Then the quiet, hesitating voice asked them all to meet in the saloon. Emergency.

The saloon was rather sardonically named: there was barely room in it for all of them, jammed together in vibrating metal and smelling each other's sweat. Alaric Wayne stood by the farther entrance, the great black dog behind him. His gauntly chiseled face was paler than before, under a tangle of mouse-brown hair, and his big light eyes did not look at any of them, but beyond. He spoke fast, impersonally:

'Miss Grenfell has plotted out for me the pattern of transaudible vibrations which indicate something is going wrong with our blast. It's changing rapidly, the pattern, but the data were enough, taken in conjunction with other observations, to give me an idea of the trouble. It's something no one could have foreseen, for no one had ever been this close to the sun.'

No, thought Collie, nobody ever had. It was hot and close in the ship. His shirt stuck wetly to his back.

'Astronomers have long suspected that the solar energy output has sharp peaks at certain levels,' continued Wayne, as dryly as if he were lecturing to a class on Earth. 'Now it turns out that it does. There is a strong emission of charged particles which can get about this far out before falling back into the solar atmosphere. They, and the secondary emissions from our hull which they cause, don't amount to enough to harm us, but they do affect the electrostatic fields which direct the ion blast. Not much, but enough so that a certain small percentage of the positive ions ejected strike their tube walls, and on the shadow side of the ship some of these, losing all kinetic energy, acquire electrons from the solar radiation and cling there. In short, we're getting an ice crust in the port tubes, and its vapors are disturbing the blast. Unless it's remedied, our tubes will shortly be eaten through.'

114

Silence.

'I – I –' Wayne looked away. 'I'm s-s-sorry.'

'Is hokay, captain,' said Ivanovitch. 'Like you say, who could know?'

'The question,' said Arakelian, 'is what to do about it.'

'Whatever we do will have to be done fast,' said Feinberg harshly. 'We need to blast almost the whole time in this sector, if we aren't going to get so close to the sun that we won't have reaction mass enough to pull free again.'

'Rotate the ship?' asked Gammony. 'Heat every side even an' boil that there ice out.'

'We can't do that while we're blasting,' said Arakelian, 'and if we fall free and rotate, it'll take too long. Those tubes are pretty heavily insulated.'

'I've thought it out,' said Wayne. 'We'll have to stop the jets, clean the crusted tubes, and mount electric coils on the outside to deflect the solar ions. It is a simple job; the only question is whether we can do it soon enough, before the ship falls hopelessly close. At an estimate, we can fall free for about twenty-four hours.'

Silence again. Then Gammony stretched himself and grinned. 'Okay, boys,' he said, 'what all is we standin' 'roun' heah for?'

Collie, Arakelian, and O'Neill were the tube-cleaning party, while the others worked to make the deflector coils. The hillman struggled into his spacesuit, cursing its awkwardness as he shivered with the need for haste. On Mars, they'd be using a simpler dress, but out here full armor was required. When the helmet clanged down, he had a moment of panicky claustrophobia. It died away, but his heart beat swiftly and the smell of rubber and oil lay flat in his nostrils.

Feinberg's delicate hands ran over oxygen tanks, pumps, cooling units, joints and clamps. 'Hurry up,' muttered Arakelian. His voice sounded tinny in the helmet radio. 'The devil with that checking.'

'Take it easy,' said Feinberg into the microphone he was wearing. 'We've taken too goddam many chances already.'

They went out into the airlock and waited while it was pumped clear. Collie watched the air-diffused light of the overhead bulb wane, until he and his companions were only sliding highlights against darkness under its glare. 'Okay,' said O'Neill. 'All clear.'

As they emerged on the outer hull, the acceleration was cut off. Collie gulped, his stomach turned a somersault and he bit his teeth together to hold it down. Suddenly he was falling, falling endlessly into a sky that was black and hideous around him, and he clawed at slick metal and sobbed.

'Easy there.' Arakelian laid a hand on his shoulder. 'Take it easy, Collie. It's harmless.'

Collie swallowed. His heart was loud in his ears. Above him, below him, around him glittered a hugeness of stars. They were on the shadow side, but he could see red and white flames seething beyond the curve of the ship, and they hurt his eyes. He swayed, gripping himself to the falling ship with magnetic soles, his toes curling uselessly. It was hard to see, the light was tricky, he could only pick out the metallic edges of the space-suits and the whitely flaring outline of the hull.

'Okay,' said Arakelian. There was steadiness in his tones; he had been on a practice flight to the moon. 'Let's take it slow. Keep the hull between you and the sun; if you have to look around its edge, slide your blinkers forward. Otherwise you'll be blind for a week, maybe forever. Don't lift one foot till the other one is planted firm on the hull, because if you should go jumping away from the ship there's nothing in God's universe that'll ever bring you back. We've got plenty of time to do this job – hours. Follow me, now.'

They shuffled toward the stern, holding hands. Collie swayed and teetered, but he could only tell that by the swinging of the stars in his faceplate. Every little movement brought dizziness, when there was no gravity to hold down the fluid in the semi-circular canals, but he was ill all the time and couldn't use that vertigo as a gauge. He hoped he wouldn't be sick in his suit. It was hard to tell if you had one foot on the hull or not. Once O'Neill made a misstep and floated gently toward the horrible stars, but Arakelian pulled him back.

When they came to the great clustered tubes, they stooped and duck-walked, creeping toward the throats. Arakelian planted a magnetic stanchion and they roped themselves to it. Then they felt easier, and swung around to peer down the mouths of the tubes. Collie couldn't see much detail in there, a shadowy hint of coils where the wan puddle of his flashlight touched.

Arakelian murmured to himself. 'Yeah. I spot some ice in there. Just a thin layer, but I guess it's what's making the trouble.' He unlimbered a stiff wire ending in a brush. 'Heh! Makes me feel like a goddam plumber. All right, let's swab 'em out.'

Collie hung in darkness, thrusting and wiping. Every time he pushed his brush forward, he went back, jerking to a halt at the end of his line. Arakelian, toward the sun-side, was too brilliant to look at. Collie gasped in the stuffiness of his suit. Lord! How long did this take?

Enormously later, Arakelian hauled himself around to inspect the tubes. Most of the ice was out; ship-rotation could boil the rest free quickly enough. His voice was a sigh of strengthless exhaustion: 'Okay, I guess that's it.'

Slowly, they pulled themselves in and unlashed their ropes and began the creeping walk back. They didn't hold hands this time, perhaps they were too tired to think of it; and somehow it had never occurred to anyone that they should be tied together. Collie's skull felt hollow.

He was not aware of his misstep till he saw O'Neill's armored form sliding past him. Then he screamed. He threshed his arms, and the stars spun a little and spun back again, then they did a huge cartwheel and he felt the radiance of the sun on him.

'Help!'

The awful thing was the slowness. Collie drifted from the ship, drifted a yard a minute maybe, turning and spinning, now the ship was there and now he faced the stars and now he threw an arm across his faceplate against the sun. His screaming echoed in the helmet, he thrust out his arms and cried, and the stars burned at him from a huge and waiting silence.

'My ankle,' shouted O'Neill. 'Grab it!'

He jumped frog-wise, away from the ship, and Arakelian clung to his shins and prayed that the magnets were strong enough. The Irishman passed by Collie, a foot out of reach, and jolted to a stop. Collie thought he could glimpse the tortured face as he went drifting by.

'Swing me around, Alec!' O'Neill held himself stiffly out-stretched. 'For God's sake!'

An inch a second, perhaps, limned in sun-fire against a million frosty stars, and Collie turning and tumbling from the ship. O'Neill's clumsy gauntlets slapped at the hillman's thigh, and both of them bounced apart, and Arakelian yelled and swung O'Neill around again.

This time Collie felt the gloves slam on his boot, and he waited rigidly for O'Neill's lanky form to straighten out. When the small shock of halting came, if it was great enough to tear that insecure grasp loose, he, Collie, would fall into the sun.

And Lois, whom O'Neill loved, had been holding Collie's hands, and Collie was the most dispensable man aboard, and it would be the easiest thing in the universe to let go and say he had torn loose after all. Collie jammed his teeth together and waited.

The recoil of stopping jarred him, ever so faintly, and then the hands were rising, ankle, calf, thigh, arms about his waist, and his feet clashed on metal and he swayed and sobbed against the ship.

'Jesus – Christ!' muttered Arakelian. 'Don't *ever* do that!'

Collie's throat felt like dry sand, and the shaking was on him now, but he managed to whisper that he was sorry.

'Oh, hell, it could happen to anybody,' said O'Neill.

When they were back in the ship, taking off their suits, Collie's eyes met the Irishman's, and they looked at each other for a long time.

'I got a lot to thank you for,' said Collie at last.

'Isn't anything,' said O'Neill. 'Nothing at all.'

118

9

Mars filled half the sky. When you looked out the ports on that side, the planet's ruddy-amber glow spilled in and tinted faces a strange hue. Collie's eyes followed the trace of stony hills and iron deserts, polar bogs and thin harsh equatorial scrub, the huge outline of a dust storm scudding redly over a thousand square miles of a barrenness, and it seemed impossible that this could be another world. That it would be as hard and real under his feet as the hills of Earth, and Earth herself no more than a star.

The spaceship swung in a hurrying orbit some thousand miles above the turning surface, and instruments strained forward to know what it was that waited there. High-powered telescopes, spectroscopes, thermocouples, a scribble of notes for which Schiaparelli or Lowell would have traded their lives. There was no gravity on the ship, you hung endlessly falling in a silence that after the rocket-bellowing approach maneuvers was ghostly. Voices dropped unawares to a whisper, and the small blowing of ventilators seemed unnaturally loud against that stiffness.

Collie heard Feinberg speaking: 'Seems to be about what the astronomers have thought for a long time. Perhaps a little more oxygen than was detected from Earth or the space stations, but certainly not enough to breathe. Temperatures ranging from chilly to goddam cold. Pretty flat, a few low ranges of hills. Fairly well-developed plant life, probably involving some elaborate symbiosis, but nothing like a terrestrial forest or meadow. A few tiny lakes, especially around the poles, but otherwise it's bone-dry. No sign of intelligent life, or animals of any kind, though I imagine there are some small ones. All in all, we seem to have picked a pretty grim place.'

'It beats the moon,' said Arakelian. 'Not by a great length, I admit.'

'It can be colonized,' said Wayne. 'I'm s-s-s-certain of that.'

Feinberg went back to his work, the preparation of a map. It was a big job, with all the detail they had and the necessity of tying everything in with the coordinate system established by Earth's astronomers. And doing such a task in free fall was not especially simple. Papers and instruments kept floating out of reach.

Collie turned from the room, he was no use here, and pulled himself by handholds down toward the saloon. Ivanovitch, Gammony, and Lois Grenfell were playing poker there. 'Hi,' said the negro. 'Come on an' sit in.' They had taken along no cash – hardly of use out here! – but played for I.O.U.'s which, in the weeks of journeying, had run into considerable amounts. 'Come lose yo' shirt, boy.'

'Huh,' grinned Ivanovitch. 'Lois is de one who ought to lose her shirt.'

The girl flushed, bit her lip, and said nothing. Collie felt a brief anger. Damn it, Misha had no business making such japes. She was a fine girl. She'd been together with Collie a lot since they left the sun behind, and O'Neill had withdrawn into a silent unhappiness.

Collie shoved the words back into his throat. This was no time to quarrel, however sick of the same faces you might get. It didn't seem right, either, that they should sit thumbing greasy cards while the human race, in their persons, was reaching out for the stars.

Only what in hell should you do? Heroic speeches and blowing trumpets would have been still more out of place. Man just wasn't that kind of animal.

Wasn't – hadn't been – There was no telling what man might become, in the long night of change which lay before him. Collie repressed that train of thought, it had tormented him enough, and hooked a leg about a stanchion. Taking the magnetized pencil off the table and a sheet of paper from a spindle, he scrawled a '$500' and his name and slapped the I.O.U. onto a light adhesive surface fastened to the wall. 'Okay,' he said. 'Deal me in.'

They came down out of the night and stars, riding a jet of fire and waking dim echoes in rusty valleys. Gammony, O'Neill, and Arakelian piloted them, less a team than a single trained unit, stretching its senses to make up for the lacking instruments. And when they set down, it was in a storm of sand blown up by their rockets, so that the landscape blurred for them and they wondered, briefly, if the ship would be fused here forever.

Then the tripod found bedrock, the blast died, an engine hummed to lengthen one leg enough to put the ship even, and there was silence. They had arrived.

No one said a word. It was too big for talking. Lois' hand stole into Collie's, and their fingers held closely together. The rest climbed from their acceleration harnesses and stood unmoving, unspeaking, while the silence grew around them.

Wayne spoke from the bridge. His tone was flat, not quite steady. 'Come on. Let's go outside.'

Slowly, saying little, they climbed into their airsuits. These were stiff, insulated coveralls with sliding joints and transparent helmets, holding oxygen-enriched air at ten pounds' pressure, but there was much thought behind them. The color was scarlet, luminous at night, to help if a man should get lost. Heating coils ran through the fabric, and a small, highly efficient rotary pump sucked in the Martian air, compressing and warming it enough so that a man might breathe; though there were supplementary tanks of oxygen on their backs for ordinary use.

On the shoulders was mounted a receiver for the power-beam which transmitted ship's energy to the suit, as well as the sender of a feedback radio signal which kept the separate beams pointing at the men as they moved about. With the equipment and their own mass, they weighed a little more under Mars gravity than they had done naked at home, but they could at least travel freely within a wide circle about the ship.

They held back, letting Alaric Wayne go first, but he didn't notice the gesture. He climbed down the ladder from the airlock, his dog – almost comic in its own suit – scrambling awkwardly after. Looking down, Collie saw those two as small and lonely figures, dark against the tawny, rust-streaked desolation around them.

When his own boots touched Martian ground, he stood for a long while, withdrawn into his own thoughts. Behind him, the ship was a tall steely pillar, looking up against a night-blue sky which became a thin chill greenish on the horizon. Underfoot was hard-packed sand, yielding little to his footsteps, rolling in great dunes as far as he could see. There was scant wind here to pile it up, but what there was had had millions of years to work. The ground was a dull blend of colors, yellow and ocher and dun; here and there a mineral-streaked rock lifted above the desert, its shadow black and knife-edged.

The horizon curved sharply off, and in the tenuous air seemed even nearer than it was, as if the planet had closed walls in on them. The sun was slipping westward, a small pale disc spilling wan light over the empty world. Collie could just make out the zodiacal lens which had been so clear in space, and a few of the brighter stars glittered overhead by day. He couldn't see Earth, and somehow that made his loneliness all the greater.

It was very quiet here. The purr of his compressor, the sound of his own lungs and pulse, seemed to override whatever Mars might be whispering to welcome him. Straining, he thought he could hear the tiniest voice of wind, streaming over more leagues of death than he knew. Lois, he thought, was the only one to whom Mars could really speak. Their eyes met behind glassy masks, and they smiled at each other with a certain forlornness.

'Over there.' O'Neill's words came flatly in his earphones. 'A clump of trees –'

'Mars' equivalent of a tropical jungle,' grunted Arakelian. 'Well, let's go have a look, shall we?'

They went plodding over the sand, strung out so that one man would be close to the ship. It seemed a meaningless precaution. This was not a place of wild beasts and hostile savages: Mars' threat was something older and stronger and more patient. Mars would suck the air from broken helmet and ripping lungs, would freeze a man's blood in his living veins, would gaunt him with hunger and shrivel him with thirst and take a thousand years to bury his mummified corpse under the slowly marching sands. *And this is the world we have to conquer!*

The wood was not large, a few acres of low, twisted gray trees with umbrella-sized leaves of dull green, intermingled with several kinds of dry moss-like vegetation, rust-colored lichenous patches, and pale hard fungoid growths. None of the shapes looked much like anything on Earth – it was a surrealistic nightmare till you got used to it.

Still – life! Here in rust and rock, under a rainless heaven and a niggard sun, millions of miles from Earth the lovely, there was something that lived. Collie touched the rough gray surface of a tree with a kind of reverence. Life was a frail thing, a short pale flicker in the wheeling immensity of an inorganic universe, but it could fight for its place; torn and crippled on one world, it could reach out to another and find that its own spirit had gone before. Somehow that ugly little tree became a thing of hope, and very beautiful.

'We'll take specimens – analyze, try to work out the life cycle.' Feinberg's tones seemed to come from far away.

'The scientific team can do that,' nodded Wayne. 'Meanwhile the rest of you can be setting up camp. The sooner we get our base established, the better.'

They went back to the ship. No question of taking the day off, it had to be work from the start if they were to live. But they did break out some special items for supper that night, including a few bottles of old wine, and had a little feast. In the reduced air pressure, they all got drunk. Wayne and O'Neill remained moody, but the others laughed and sang and clinked glasses again and again in the first toast, which Lois had given and which was still the only one for this proud evening.

'Well, gentlemen – we made it.'

10

The days and the nights swept over them, pale frosty light over worn-out hills and scudding dust, flash and glitter of a hundred thousand stars in a high vault of dark crystal, and always the working and the hoping. There was so much to do, and so few tools to do it with, that men lurched back into the ship at sundown and swallowed a quick meal and tumbled into beds and uneasy dreams.

It seemed to Collie that he had been forever cased in the clammy, stinking prison of his airsuit, it seemed that the tall mountains of Earth were themselves a dream he had had long ago, and that there was only the red dust and the shovel in his hands. Incredible that he had been merely weeks on Mars.

The scientific team – Wayne, Arakelian, and Feinberg – were tackling the ecology, dissecting, analyzing, theorizing, slowly completing a picture of the chemistry and the multiple symbiosis which kept those woods and grasses in existence. Lois Grenfell was cook and housekeeper and girl-of-all-work. The rest of them were building their base, and even in Martian gravity that was an inhuman job.

Slowly it grew. The ship herself had been designed so that much of her could be taken out and made into shelters, caches, and equipment, leaving only a skeletal minimum for the trip home; and her cargo held the knocked-down parts which were otherwise required. For lack of building materials, most of Port Drummond was underground, merely excavated and roofed over; but a junkyard of material littered the acres around the ship, and the ancient dun of Mars was interrupted by a fierce new gleam of naked metal.

The next expedition could carry supplies to put in those vaults, and the one after that could leave a few men to carry on the work, and the one after that – God in Heaven! How long would it take to get even one tiny village going, fifty million miles from home?

Collie and Ivanovitch suffered less from their working conditions than the other laborers. The Russian's immense strength left him breathing easily, while the hillman's peculiar lung and blood system made him less prone to stagger and claw for air. But Collie was the only one of those two who took a real interest in the work as a problem, rather than merely a job; and thus, gradually and unintentionally, he found himself a kind of foreman.

Damn it, there was a challenge here. In their favor, they had the low gravity and the loose, friable earth; against them was the same crumbly texture, with its tendency to collapse, and the incredible dryness. Ordinary concrete wouldn't set decently, before it had dried the ravenous dust had sucked half the water from it and you got a flimsy stuff which the erosion of temperature extremes would soon ruin. So you devised molds of plastic board which would act as a shield till the concrete was properly set. One of the furtive, tiny animals chewed the insulation off power lines, so you had to bury them in concrete too. Then you ran out of cement and had to scout around looking for some local substitute: a clay which mixed with water and baked into bricks.

But you couldn't spend water that lavishly, so you had to find it elsewhere, you had to extract it from the fluid-hoarding cells of certain trees. Quickly growing rootlets with some unknown dowsing sense would split open any pipe or container with moisture in it, so you had to eradicate all plants for miles around and lay the pipes in open tunnels where they could be inspected. And on, and on, and on.

And slowly the base was growing. A score of interconnected cellars, Wayne's sunpower accumulators on their roofs, a shielded excavation for the nuclear power-pile which the next expedition would install, greenhouses for plants to renew oxygen and supply a little food, adumbrations of laboratories and storehouses. It was a tiny thing, lost in rolling drab immensities, and it was bare and bleak and primitive, but it grew. It grew. Sometimes, straightening for a moment and casting his weary eyes over the litter, Collie felt a resurgence of that first pride when they landed. He thought he could see Port Drummond a hundred years from now, and it was a tall white city and the desert around it was becoming green.

There was no warning of what followed. To them, Mars was enemy enough, and they had not thought the old hatreds of Earth would hunt them this far. But there came an evening.

Collie glanced at the declining sun and called a halt. As soon as it was down, night and the stars would explode over them. 'Dinner time, I reckon,' he said.

The dog, which had been hauling a girder, stopped in his harness and sat down, waiting to be untied. Collie often wondered just how intelligent the brute was. He labored with them, taking simple orders and not needing to be driven, but still – something uncanny there. He wasn't a dog you patted and called 'nice fellow' . . .

The other men brought their tools to the chest and laid them inside, a precaution against dust storms that might cover them. Their grotesque suited forms were etched black against the sky, with long shadows pointing at the ship. Ivanovitch remained a moment on the job, tightening a last pipe joint, and then clumped after the others. Collie stood for a moment alone, glancing over the hills, wondering what lay beyond that barren horizon. More of the same, probably. No golden castles, no beautiful princesses, just Mars. This was a world to which man had to bring his own dreams.

Something flashed out there, in the last sunlight, a hard metal gleam. He squinted, scowling into the glare, and thought he saw it move. What the devil?

Imagination, I reckon, he told himself, and turned back toward the airlock. The hatefully familiar walls closed around him. He wrinkled his nose at the faint staleness inside the ship, they could never quite get rid of it.

Shucking his suit and hanging it in the lock, he made his way to the tiny bathroom and waited his turn to sponge off some of the sweat. Feinberg was ahead of him, talking excitedly to an unresponsive O'Neill: 'Yeah, the goddam plant gets oxygen out of rocks. Some organic catalyst, I don't know what it is, but out the oxy comes in a loose chemical bond. With a little selective breeding, we might get something really efficient for our colony: plants that refine iron ore for us and give us air and have edible tubers into the bargain. But first we'll have to work out the laws of heredity. The chromosome pattern doesn't look like anything I ever saw on Earth, and we can't assume that it'll follow the same Mendelian laws we know.'

Collie wiped himself halfway clean, donned his inboard clothes, and strolled down to the saloon. Most of the others were already seated, staring glumly at their plates, too weary to talk. What was the use of talking, anyway, when you knew exactly what the other fellow had to say on any imaginable subject?

Lois came in from the tiny gallery with a bowl of stew. Collie thought that she was the only goodlooking object on the whole planet. Her thin straight face was flushed with the heat of the little stove, her eyes were bright and the soft brown hair curled down over her shoulders. Collie thought he'd like to run his hands through that hair. But it wouldn't do, it wouldn't do. Maybe later, sometime on the other side of eternity, when they got back to Earth.

'M-m-m-m,' he said. 'Smells nice, that mulligan.'

She checked off an imaginary number. 'That makes ninety-seven times you've said that,' she answered, but smiled at him.

'Well,' said Collie, 'I gotta say something.'

'Forty-three.'

'Okay, okay, I give up. You're beautiful.'

'Fifty-one.' She set the bowl down in front of him.

O'Neill looked grayly at them. Collie felt a twinge of remorse. He had no business stirring up a fresh dispute.

'I saw something which looked like metal today,' Collie said, to change the subject. 'Just a flash out in the west, as I was comin' in.'

'Ah,' said Feinberg. 'The Martians have found us.'

'No, really.' Lois looked interested. 'What could it have been? A lake out there?'

'No,' said Gammony. 'Not accordin' to the maps we made, it can't be. Mebbe a bright rock the dust just blew off of.'

At another time, they might have speculated in great detail, merely to talk about something. Tonight the matter died.

Collie felt restless after dinner. Most of the others were off to their bunks; Wayne and Feinberg went back to the ship's lab, Arakelian and O'Neill started a drowsy game of chess. The hillman yawned. 'I'm goin' out for a stroll,' he said to nobody in particular.

'Don't you get enough of that damned desert?' grumbled Arakelian.

'It's nice at night,' said Collie defensively.

Lois looked up from her book. They had taken a microviewer and a good-sized filmed library along, it was worth its weight in oxygen to them. 'I'll come along, if you don't mind,' she said.

Collie's heart sprang. 'Sure,' he said.

O'Neill shoved the chessboard from him with a savage gesture. 'I concede,' he said. 'I'm off to my bunk.'

The worst of it for the poor guy, thought Collie, *is that he can't even keep his feelings private.* He lost pity in a rush of his own emotions, not unmixed with a certain smugness.

When he and Lois stepped out, the night was on them in one huge wintry blaze of stars. The desert lay dim under heaven, fading into illimitable immensities, nothing moving, nothing speaking. The sound of their own feet, scrunching on hard-packed sand, was loud in their ears. His hand stole out and took hers as they walked from the ship.

'I wish,' he said at last, clumsily, 'we didn't have to go around in these here suits.'

'Why?' she asked.

'You know why,' he said.

'It's just as well,' she answered.

'Lois –'

'No, Collie,' she said. 'We can't afford to have private lives. Not here. Don't talk. Isn't it a wonderful sight, that sky?'

He bit his lip and felt his face grow hot. It was always like this. He'd tried to kiss her, once or twice when they were briefly alone, but she wouldn't have it. She wouldn't talk of that tomorrow when they were again on Earth. And the hell of it was, she was right.

Her face was a pale highlighting against darkness. His eyes followed the curve of cheek and nose and lips, he saw the glimmer of starlight in hair and eyes, and he could only look. *Damn it*, he thought, *damn it. I should of stayed home.*

The stillness closed around them. They walked around the

edge of the camp, looking at the high cold stars and the wolf-gray desert, not speaking, not even thinking much.

Collie started when Lois' free hand caught his arm. 'Stop!' she whispered.

He paused, staring blankly at her. She was standing in a crouched position, her head cocked behind the helmet, and the starlight was a blind shimmer in her eyes. Listening.

'What –'

'Quiet,' she breathed. 'Quiet – something out there.'

He raised a hand to cup his ear, and felt it strike the helmet. There was nothing. No sound, no stir, only the small hiss of his own breathing. But she heard, and grasped his arm with a new urgency.

'Something in the camp – some animal – come on!'

'No!' He pulled her back. 'This's my business.'

He glided forward, slipping from shadow to shadow. The awkwardness of the suit didn't hamper him too much, it was almost like stalking in the mountains again. But his heartbeat grew noisy within him, and he strained through the half-light and felt his gloves turn wet on the inside. What the devil – Mars didn't have any big animals!

No, wait, now he heard it too, the faintest mutter in the sound-deadening air, a clink and thump there among the skeleton forms of girders and machines. He went down on his belly and snaked forward, around the edge of a low wall.

Men!

Four men stood there, watching the ship from the shelter of a big packing case. Strangers! Even though they were only a dim flow of starlight along metal and plastic, he knew them for strangers. And he saw the gleam of a gun barrel.

Something hard and cold knotted in his stomach. He crouched, wondering how long they had been here, wondering if they had seen him and Lois come out, wondering who they were and what they wished. Even as he lay staring, he saw them advance cautiously, around the case and toward the tall gray pillar of the ship.

If they're friends, he thought somewhere in his hammering brain, *why're they sneakin' up on us like that? And if they're enemies – Christ, but we're alone out here!*

It was not courage, or even recklessness, but a cold, half-instinctive realization that he had nothing to lose, which drove him forward. He was up from the ground in one long leap, surging toward the four, and as he hit them he shouted to Lois that she must warn the others

The men whirled as he struck them. He thought blindly and wildly that he was unarmed, he had to mix it in with them and not give them a chance to shoot. But what good were fists and feet and teeth when everyone wore armor? Then he had his arms around one and was grappling him, bumping into the rest, kicking and cursing and yelling for help.

In a brief lifting from shadow, his opponent's face was flat and slant-eyed, Mongoloid, and he thought: *Siberians!* Then a pair of gigantic hands plucked him free and lifted him into the air.

He hung threshing in a grip as immense as Ivanovitch's, beating his fists down on the helmet and the bearded face underneath. Guns must be swiveling on him now. He twisted about and kicked with both feet at the air pump on the giant's back. Once, twice, three times with his abnormal leg muscles, and the casing broke open and the Siberian roared and flung him to the ground.

He bounced up as a slug spirited past. With a huge leap, he butted his helmet into the rifleman's belly. They went over together, and Collie got the rifle and rolled free.

He snapped a shot at another shadow. A stream of bullets stitched fire in the night, reaching for him. He sprang backward, landing in an open pit. The Siberians plunged after him, halting on the edge and shooting blind into it, but he was out again. Crouching on the bank, he fired with better aim, and one of the men screamed. His moisture-laden air streamed from his punctured suit, ghost white in the savage cold, and he fell into the pit.

Rolling behind the banked earth, Collie lay waiting for their next move. Wouldn't the others ever come? Did it take them that long to get their suits on? They had a few guns aboard, not having been sure there were no wild beasts on Mars. What were the remaining Siberians up to now?

A stream of lead hosed at him from one side. They'd circled about. Collie fired at the vague shape and scrambled up and ran for shelter. The bullets chewed after him as he zigzagged.

Fire blazed from the ship. A dashing figure, a hammering tommy-gun, rescue! Suddenly the two living Siberians were in retreat. They sped over the desert, running and running, and the night drank them up.

Collie fell to his hands and knees, sucking air into starved lungs. He couldn't get enough, he was choking, horror seized him and his mind whirled into darkness.

He must only have been out a minute or two. When he looked up, Lois was bending over him. There was a submachine-gun in her hand. 'Collie,' she breathed. 'Collie, are you all right?'

'Yeah – yeah.' He sat up, aided by her. He was still alive. Incredibly, his suit had not been punctured, he still had breath and vision and motion. He felt utterly empty of strength. 'I'm . . . okay. But where's the rest?'

'They'll be along as soon as they can. It takes time to put on these damned suits. I went in and warned them, then took this gat and came out again.'

'Good girl.' A little energy was returning to him, though he still felt light-headed. 'Help me up, huh?'

He leaned on her and they walked slowly back toward the ship. *A few good breaths*, he thought, *a couple lungfuls of air, that's all I need. I'm still alive.*

They passed the giant. A seven-footer he was, lying stark on the sand with the starlight icy in his eyes. No air pump, no air, he must have strangled quickly. And the other one, the man in the pit, would also be dead, his blood freezing as the cold slid in through his torn suit. Neither of them would talk, not ever again.

Collie bent over the giant. On his back was a massive bazooka tube and a rack of rocket shells. 'What did they want?' asked Lois. There was a sob in her voice, now that the immediate danger was past. 'What were they after?'

'To put a hole in our ship, I reckon,' said Collie. 'Quick way to kill us all off.'

'But why?' She clung to him, and he held her close through the stiff fabric. '*Why?*'

He shrugged, grinning lopsidedly to hide the terror that rose in him. 'I reckon they just don't like us,' he said.

11

Alaric Wayne stood facing them. The saloon was hot and close with the heavy breathing of men, it was full of the smell of fear. The dog bristled and showed his teeth at the sharp odor of their fright. They were very quiet, watching the captain. The overhead light glared on them, throwing eyes and cheeks and throats into pits of shadow, until it was like a rank of skulls watching him. And they waited.

'I –I –' He groped after words, but there was only a hollowness in him. 'I do n-n-not know wh-what to s-s-s-s – say. This is a surprise to me too, and, well, a surprise.'

'The question,' said Feinberg sharply, 'is what we are going to do about it.'

'They are Siberians?' asked Gammony. His voice was low and heavy. 'They really are?'

'*Da,*' said Ivanovitch. 'Marks in Rosshian on deir equipment.'

'And one of the dead men is of Asian race,' added Feinberg. 'Yeah, our friends are Siberians all right. And what does that mean?' When there was no reply, he answered himself: 'An expedition of their own. It may have taken off a little earlier or a little later than ours, depending on what orbit and accelerations they used, but at any rate it got here later, probably not many days ago.'

'How d'you figure that?' asked O'Neill.

'Because they knew just where we were. That means they spotted us from space, while making their preliminary studies. And if they're so eager to dispose of us, they wouldn't have lost any time in making the attempt. Nor can their ship – or ships – be too far from ours, since their men could get here on foot.'

'Maybe they got some kind of cars,' ventured Collie.

'Not when every pound of mass counts,' declared Feinberg. 'No, I don't see that. They had power-beam receivers similar to our own, as well as batteries to carry them a ways beyond beam range. The implication is that their spies – or intelligence agents, if you want the polite word – have lifted the knowledge of power-beaming from our country. Quite probably they got a good many tips on spaceship building from our project too, if not the complete plans. They must have *known* we were coming here.'

'Well,' said Wayne, 'it wasn't a secret.'

'No,' said Feinberg, 'but when they start out at practically the same time as we, it's more than coincidence. Goddammit, they came here with the main idea of liquidating us!'

'Why?' There was a strange helplessness on Wayne's face. 'Why should they do that?'

'Their government don't like ours,' said Arakelian, 'and also, if they knock us out, they'll have all our equipment and installations. We'll have done a lot of their hauling and work for them, if they plan to set up a Mars colony of their own.'

'There's room for everyone,' said Lois. 'Great God, do we have to carry our stupid quarrels out here too?'

'For some reason,' shrugged Arakelian, 'Siberia must want a monopoly on Mars. Just why doesn't matter right now. What counts is doing something about it.'

'And that something,' said O'Neill, 'is to get the hell out of here. If they came prepared to fight us, they'll have all the advantages. We'd best go home and be reporting the matter while we can.'

Ivanovitch shook his head, and there was anger in the blue eyes. 'No,' he growled. 'Give dem deir own medicine back. We can do it. We ain't cowards.'

O'Neill flushed. 'Take that back!' he snapped. 'I was just after saying what the sensible thing would be.'

'That's enough, boys,' said Arakelian. 'Nobody's calling you yellow, Tom. Me, I kind of think you're right. The information is more important than any heroics.'

'And once they're in possession here, and have had time to build up defenses, just how do we get our port back?' challenged Feinberg. 'Lug tanks and battleships clear from Earth, I suppose?'

'Wait – wait!' Alaric Wayne held up one thin hand. It seemed to trew silence.

'Economics –' He paused and drew a long breath. 'It seems

best to me to stay here for a while, at least. We are warned now, and can make our own defenses. I could build a colloid resonator like I once did – nobody ever was told how it works. Yes, I think we could stand them off, since they can hardly have aircraft along and a spaceship is not made for bombing.'

O'Neill grinned harshly. 'That puts a different light on it,' he said. 'Faith, we can mop 'em up ourselves!'

'Not so easily,' said Wayne. He spoke low and tonelessly, looking at the floor. 'We are eight, and they must be many more. The resonator is a weapon of limited value. I would have to think!' He glanced back up at them with a curious pleading. 'I am not a magician. I cannot pull invincibility out of a hat. This situation will have to be evaluated, and for that we need information.'

'Scouts,' nodded Gammony. 'Yeah, sho' thing. Count me in.'

Wayne shook his head. 'It is not a matter for volunteers,' he replied. 'We must make up the optimum party.'

Collie stole a look at Lois. She was giving the captain a withdrawn and bitter stare, and he knew what she was thinking. *Cogs in a machine.*

'It'll be a dangerous job,' said Arakelian. 'They'll be expecting us to try it.'

'But this is a large territory, and it gets rugged toward the west, where they fled,' answered Wayne. 'Mr. Collingwood, your special inheritance, plus your hunter's background, seem to single you out for leader.'

Collie nodded, not trusting himself to speak. He was scared, sure, he hated the thought of going out where there were guns, but –

'Then Mr. Ivanovitch, whose strength will prove valuable on an arduous march,' continued Wayne, 'and Mr. O'Neill, who can spy out details from a distance without requiring binoculars whose reflections could betray him, and Miss Grenfell, who could detect possible ambushes or the like. The rest of us will prepare defenses.'

'Hey, now, wait!' O'Neill stepped forward, pushing by the others. 'You can't send Lois to –'

'It's all right, Tom,' she said, almost in a whisper. 'I'd like to go.'

'But – but –'

'You heard her, Mr. O'Neill,' said Wayne coldly. 'Now, Mr. Collingwood, obviously I can't give you any specific instructions.

Just do what you can. Value your lives above everything else – each of you is one-eighth of our fighting strength – and do nothing reckless. I would suggest that you scouts get some sleep now, while the rest of us make up your equipment for you.'

Just like that, thought Collie. *Just like that.*

Dawn was swift on Mars, pale cold light climbing rapidly into the sky and then suddenly the bitter day. When Collie emerged, the changeless desert was already etched hard to the near horizon. He had a brief wistful remembrance of dawns on Earth, for a moment it was as if he stood again in grass that was wet with dew and listened to the chatter of birds in high trees, then he jerked his mind back and nodded to the others. 'Let's go,' he said.

Four human forms, clumsy in their airsuits, walked out across the desert, and the rest stood watching till they were gone from sight. Collie turned the situation over in his head. The power-beam wouldn't help them much past the horizon, but they had extra batteries and sun-power accumulators which would recharge those to some degree. They were all heavily burdened with food and water. Ivanovitch's pack was almost as big as himself, and had weapons. Allowing a reasonable safety margin, they could keep going for six days, three out and three back. The Siberians could be no farther away: the chances were it was only about two days' march to their ship.

Their trail was clear enough to his hunter's eyes. In this quiet air, even dust-tracks were slow to disappear. He noted landmarks and the positions of the sun and visible stars, without conscious effort. To the untrained vision, Mars looked all the same – rusty dunes, color-streaked out-croppings of rock, gnarled thickets, steep ravines, the distant swelling of low hills. But he should be able to find his way back.

O'Neill spoke after a while. Voices had a curiously tinny sound as they came through the speakers, the air, and the earphones. 'Won't they be knowing we'll follow?'

'Mebbe,' shrugged Collie. 'Not much they can do 'bout it, though, 'cept try to bushwhack us, an' that wouldn't be easy in this open country.'

'I mean, how about their evading us? Crossing bare rock, for instance, where they won't leave a trail?'

135

'They went back along the way they come—see the two sets o' prints? We can always follow the first trail. An' since it ain't too easy to locate y'rself here, they prob'ly just took a compass bearin' an' headed in a straight line f'r our camp. So far both trails point due north-northwest. No, we'll locate 'em all right.'

Lois bit her lip. 'I still can't understand it,' she murmured. 'This world is enough of an enemy for the whole human race. Why do we have to fight each other as well?'

'Dey started it,' said Ivanovitch.

'No, I mean, well, it's as if there were something wrong with all humankind. As if we could never learn.'

'Some people,' said Collie, 'don't. Not without a club to teach 'em.'

'It isn't that simple,' said O'Neill. 'We have to strike back, in self-defense, so that's how this particular battle gets started. But why did they attack us in the first place? It isn't that they're monsters. They have some other purpose, a high purpose for which they'll fight anything – Mars or their fellow men or the whole universe. And I'm thinking that a race which wouldn't fight for what it considered worthwhile, wouldn't last long.'

'So what do we do?' asked Lois desolately. 'Do we just keep on tearing each other's throats out, till the end of time?'

'We change the purposes,' said O'Neill. 'We give the entire human race the same goals.'

'Hard to do,' grunted Collie. 'Won't even be a single race any more.'

'It's got to be done,' said O'Neill. For a moment, he looked beyond them, and there was a dream on his face.

Collie shrugged again and fell silent. They marched on. The ship had vanished over the horizon, and they were alone among rocks and dunes and quietness.

The ordinary processes of living became fantastically complicated here. You ate a cold meal by attaching a box, with gasketed holes for your hands, to the helmet, and opening a special port between helmet and box – *feed bag*, thought Collie sardonically. You drank a careful ration of water through a nippled hose that plugged to a water tank. You answered the calls of nature by going behind a dune with a special apparatus to protect you from loss of air and heat.

You could do nothing about sweat and a growing beard, so you were always aware of itching and had no way to scratch. Your very breathing depended on tanks and valves and pumps, here your body was only the dependent part of a machine. It had not been so bad around camp, with the ship always at hand, but out in the desert, with nothing to do but walk, madness began to gnaw; you knew your unreasoning irritation for its first tooth-marks and there was little you could do to control it.

'It's too big for us,' said Collie. 'We'll never lick Mars. We can't take on a whole planet.'

'We've got to,' said O'Neill.

'Oh, sure, we can talk about ways and means. But we can't bring enough people, enough machinery, enough anything. It'd be a lot easier to colonize the South Pole.'

'That it would,' said O'Neill, except that the Antarctic happens to be radioactive. We've no choice. We *must* have Mars.'

'Have it – how? By diggin' pits in the ground?'

'For a starter, yes. And after that building colonies around and over the pits. Then modifying terrestrial and Martian lifeforms, and improving our biochemistry and algae farming, so the colonies are self-supporting. Then getting some more oxygen into the atmosphere – there's a lot of it locked up in these rocks – and water, and carbon dioxide; and meanwhile, perhaps, working towards a race of colonists who don't need so much air and heat as true Earthlings. Then bit by bit, decade by decade for the next five hundred or a thousand years, reclaiming these deserts. It can be done. The fundamental knowledge is already ours. What we need is engineering practice, and money, and work. Always work.'

'Money,' said Collie. 'Hell, ain't no country on Earth, ain't all Earth herself, can pay for that.'

'They'll have to,' said O'Neill. 'Money is just a symbol for human effort. If the whole race of man has to give up everything for a century, live on a bare survival level, to start a successful Mars colony, then it'll just have to, that's the whole of it. Because it's a matter of all life surviving. We've *got* to have research stations free of contamination, and unmutated Martian life to experiment with, before we can learn enough genetics to unscramble our heredity. And if that fails, if the job can't be done, then Earth's ecology will go to hell, only the most primitive animals will live. Then Mars is still the only hope: the Mars colonists will keep going, and eventually they'll come back to reseed Earth with life.' He shook his dark head. 'Survival is not a money matter, Collie.'

The hillman glanced at him. *Funny,* he thought, *I never figured Tom for a fighter. And yet he's more so than me, in his own way.*

'Yeah,' he said aloud. 'Yeah, I reckon you're right. But when we get home, if we ever do, I'm not liftin' my a – um – myself off Earth till they're carryin' my coffin.'

'I'll stay here,' said O'Neill quietly. 'Earth may be more comfortable just now, but Mars is where there is hope.'

Lois gave him a long stare, her eyes traveled over to Collie and then back to him again. 'First,' she said practically, 'there's the little matter of these Siberians.'

They pitched camp in a hollow between two dunes. A shovel made a shallow pit in which they erected the heavy fabric, half tent and half sleeping bag, that was their only shelter. It was hoped that the body heat of four people huddled together would be enough so that only a small drain on the batteries was needed.

It grew cold in the night, grimly and unrelentingly cold. The moisture of their breathing made a thick, spongy coating of ice inside the fabric, ice they would scrape off at dawn before it volatilized and drink again. Collie kept waking up, his muscles stiff with chill, and telling himself harshly that he would *not* turn up the heating coils. He was too miserable even to be very much aware of Lois lying there beside him.

12

Collie lay on his belly, looking between two high, gnawed crags, down a long rubbly slope to the enemy camp. The waning sun was at his back, he'd circled around so it wouldn't glare off their metal, and shadows spilled hugely along the hillside and rose like liquid about the ships.

There were two of them, each a little bigger than his own, squatting on their tails amidst the iron barrenness of the little valley. A couple of airsuited figures patrolled around them, and he could make out the shapes of machine-guns mounted in stone-walled dugouts. Some machinery had been assembled outdoors, presumably to give more room within the vessels, but there was little trace of construction work.

'Yes,' muttered O'Neill at his side. 'They came here to take over our camp, all right.'

'Well, now they know they didn't,' said Collie. 'So what'll they try next?'

'Couldn't say. Ordinarily, I'd guess a frontal attack, but all the world has a healthy respect for Alaric Wayne. And there can't be more than twenty or so of them.' O'Neill's mutant eyes ranged down the hillside, studying minutiae of territory that were invisible to Collie.

'You're the boss,' O'Neill said after a while. 'What do you advise? I can't see much more than we've already spied, and it's too far away for Lois to hear anything – even if she understood Russian.'

'The safe thing,' said Collie, 'would be hightail it for home right away. But that just gives 'em more time to prepare. What I'd like to do is sneak down there with that rocketslinger we took off their man an' hole their ships like they meant to hole ours. Then we wouldn't have to worry any more about 'em, an' we'd get their supplies and stuff to boot.'

'They aren't stupid,' warned O'Neill. 'They'll have alarms rigged. I think I can just make out a couple of spots which look like they might have black-light cells buried there. A fence of UV, and if we break it to get in at them we'll be calling out the marines.'

'Hmmm – yeh. Though wait – Look, Tom, those beams'll be close to the ground. They'll expect us to come crawlin' up at them.'

'So we jump over instead, eh? And land right on top of something else.'

'It won't take long to blow holes in both ships. Then their air goes whooshin' out. I can tote the rocketslinger close enough in a matter o' seconds. They won't know how fast I can run.'

O'Neill gave him an odd look. 'You really are hell-bent to wipe them out, aren't you?' he murmured.

'Shucks, I just want to get home,' grinned Collie. 'Where I come from, we're not too finicky about our enemies' lives.'

Behind him, Lois laid a hand on his shoulder. 'No, Collie,' she said. 'They'll have sentries outside too, if they aren't utter fools. Men at the machine-guns.'

'Uh-huh,' he agreed. 'Here's how we do it. We've all got arms, an' in this thin air we don't have to move too quietly. Tom an' Misha sneak up on either side with their tommy-guns an' cut down these guards. I'll have snuck up to the black-light barrier by then. I can get that close without bein' spotted. The minute you two boys start firin', I jump the barrier, dash in close, an' put three or four rocket shells through their hulls.'

'And me?' she asked.

'You stay here.'

'Now look, just because I'm a woman –'

'Tain't that, honey. If we don't make it, somebody's got to carry word back.'

She looked at him for a long moment, and then sighed and turned away. Collie gestured O'Neill to crawl back out of sight from the camp with him.

They spent the next hour planning the operation in some detail, using O'Neill's minute knowledge of the terrain. At sundown they bolted a hasty meal, though Collie's throat felt too stiff to swallow. *Let's face it*, he thought, *I'm scared. I'm scared sweatless.*

Night came like a thunderclap. O'Neill returned from the vantage point to report that there were only two sentries, as had been guessed: one on either side of the ships, close to the machine-guns. They were fairly well placed, each could sweep a good half-circle, but the hills rose so steeply and ruggedly on every hand that an attacker could slip from shadow to shadow until he was within yards of his man. And the dulled sounds of gunfire would not penetrate a heavy insulated spaceship wall. There was no light from the ports, everyone else must be asleep.

Collie licked sandy lips. He wished he had a good slug of whiskey inside him. 'Okay,' he said, 'I'll be off. Give me fifteen minutes an' start yourselves. Good luck to us all.'

Ivanovitch rumbled something in his throat, and O'Neill clamped his shoulder briefly. Lois came to stand before them. He could just see the tremble of her lips in the starlight. 'God be with you,' she whispered, and her helmet clinked against theirs.

He couldn't help a wry grin at how the gesture must look, but it made him feel warm inside. Turning, he started off.

The stones were rough under him as he snaked down the slope, flowing toward the farther end of the Siberian camp. He went from gully to crag to dune, stopping with his heart a thunder in his ears, peering ahead to see if anything had stirred. The stars were huge and cold above him, even then he was aware of his own littleness beneath that sky. He pulled his mind back to the job. Mission: murder – rip the air from the lungs and the blood from the noses of men he had never seen, men who probably had wives and children waiting for them back on Earth. Mission: survival.

The scraping of rocks and scratching of drifted sand seemed unnaturally loud. He wondered why the whole planet didn't wake with a shriek. The captured Siberian superbazooka on his back seemed to tower against the stars, incredible that the guards didn't spy that walking skyscraper. The ships loomed like armored monsters, they had crossed between worlds and *he* was going to try and slay those firedrakes!

No. He didn't worry too much about his own end of the job. A rocket shell could punch through the light steel hulls, and its explosion would make too big a hole for the self-sealing to heal.

Three or four such holes would let out enough air so that men would choke before they could get on their suits. Captain Wayne had shown him last morning (only two days ago?) how to operate the thing, it was childishly simple to a man who had grown up using bows and homemade smoothbore muskets. He had crawled unseen up to his quarry over more difficult terrain. O'Neill had shown him exactly where the UV fence, if there was one, must be planted. A six-foot jump and a thirty-yard dash were nothing to him, even on Mars.

But the other two–they weren't scouts or soldiers. A tommy-gun wasn't the easiest weapon in the world either. It was a terrible thought that his own life rested on men who might fail.

Well –

He was almost up to the little mound where the alarm was buried. He lay flat, his dirt-rubbed suit and equipment another part of the dim landscape, and peered ahead. He could just see starlight shimmer along one machine-gun barrel. The tautness in him, the need for action, grew almost unendurable. God! What was keeping the others?

He gathered himself, crouching inside his skin, biting his jaws together as he waited.

The searchlight glare was a blow. He yelled, throwing up an arm as it found his eyes. A gun clattered, kicking up dust around him. He scrambled up and tried to run. The light and the bullets followed him. The amplified voice was like a roar of judgment.

'Surrender! Surrender or be killed! You are taken!'

He dropped to his hands and knees, sobbing, knowing he could not outrun a bullet. The firing ceased. Turning, he tried to unlimber his bazooka. A warning spurt of lead ate at the dust.

The light came from the nose of one ship. Beyond its white glare was only darkness, but he thought he could see other beams probing. And here they came, suited figures trotting from the night with guns pointed at his belly. He raised his hands and stood waiting.

One of the Siberians jerked a thumb toward the ships, while the other stood well aside, covering him. He slogged toward prison with a dry weeping in him.

As he neared the airlock, he saw O'Neill and Ivanovitch, also under guard. The Russian was cursing, a glimpse of his face showed him blind with rage and bafflement. Collie couldn't make out O'Neill's visage, but even through the heavy suit it could be seen how his shoulders were bent.

'They're out after Lois,' he said tonelessly. 'A bunch of them just ran by, headed for her.'

'But how did they –'

'I don't know. It doesn't matter.'

Presently the girl was brought back. She moved wearily, breathing hard. She must have tried to flee, but they had run her down. One of her captors had abnormally long legs.

A man gestured at the retractable ladder. They went up it and stood in the airlock. The usual blindness engulfed them as moisture froze on suits and helmets. Hands fumbled at Collie, trying to get his suit off. He batted them aside. 'I can undress myself,' he said dully.

He felt strangely helpless and without dignity, standing there in the one-piece undergarment. A good dozen men clustered about them, similarly clad. Ivanovitch growled, bear-like, and doubled his fists. Someone else grinned at him: a dark fellow, big as he, but with four arms, one pair behind the other.

Something of the numbness lifted from Collie as he was urged down a short corridor. He looked about him. The ship had the same metallic bleakness as his own, though here it was unrelieved by the murals which Feinberg had painted to while away the trip. The men around were about half of white, half of Oriental stock, and all had sidearms. They revealed several mutations: the long legs, the size and double arm, the supple extra-jointed fingers, and probably many more which didn't show on the outside. A crew of favourables, just like the Americans. But there were some differences which seemed neither handicap nor asset: a hairless skull, oddly placed ears and nose, long webbed toes on one set of bare feet. The Siberians must have been less fussy.

The prisoners were shown up a companionway and into a small anteroom where a motionless sentry slanted his rifle. An order was barked, and most of the company left. The four-armed man and a Mongoloid whose quick deft movements suggested superhuman reaction-speed remained. The sentry knocked on the door, a voice answered, and the door was opened. Collie led the way inside.

It was obviously the bridge, though a desk and cabinet had been installed to make an office ot it. A searchlight battery, hastily erected to shine through the vision ports, together with some electronic apparatus Collie didn't recognize, took most of the remaining space. His eyes went to the man behind the desk.

That one smiled. 'Come in, please,' he said. 'Be seated, if you wish, though I am afraid we have only the floor to sit on. Colonel Boris Byelinsky of the Siberian Khanate, at your service.'

13

Collie paused for a long while, studying this man who held their lives between his fingers. He seemed to be around forty, though the shaven head and the broad features gave him a curiously ageless look. His stocky form was at ease but remained flawless in the gray-green uniform. The eyes were small and blue, not unkindly, and the mouth was sensitive. He spoke English with a rather mechanical perfection, no real accent of any kind to give it color.

'I think I know your names already,' he said after a pause. 'Collingwood, O'Neill, Grenfell and Ivanovitch – yes, I rather suspected it would be you four who came. But do sit down. I assure you, we have no harmful intentions.'

Slowly, Collie lowered himself till he was hunkering on the floor. The stunned feeling was leaving him, he began really to see what an unimaginable catastrophe this was, and he fought not to tremble. His voice wouldn't remain steady: 'Yeah. After you tried to kill us all!'

'No, no,' Byelinsky shook his head. 'You were the ones who thought of killing. Our men were only supposed to disable your rocket and then, when you emerged to investigate, capture you. It would be criminal to waste such stock as yours, which is so rare and precious a thing these days. Of course,' he finished gently, 'if necessary, we will shoot to kill, but I hope that the necessity will not arise.'

'Why?' It was a whisper in O'Neill's throat. 'Why fight at all? Faith, we'd no mind to harm you if you wished to colonize.'

'That,' said Byelinsky, 'is a question of national policy. You might almost say the problem is philosophical.' He gestured at the searchlights. 'Please do not think us altogether incompetent. When our men came back with their story of failure, we knew we could expect a vist from you, and guessed pretty closely what its nature would be. So we made preparations. We have a person aboard with ears at least as sensitive as yours, Miss Grenfell, and it was a simple matter to install this microphone pickup so that he could hear every sound outside for a kilometer or more. There were armed, suited men waiting just inside the air lock, and these lights to pick you out. It was as simple as that.'

'Yeah.' Collie looked at the floor. As simple as that. And he'd walked right into it. He, the great scout, the hunter, the expert, he'd blundered into it like a bear into a deadfall. He clenched his fists and felt tears sting his eyes. This was no place for him, he wasn't fit to meet the world, he wanted to go home.

'There remains the problem of your comrades,' said Byelinsky. 'But several possibilities for dealing with them occur to me. We have at least one gun which can shell them from a good range. Once their ship is holed, they will soon have to surrender. However, I would prefer a more workman-like method. One which did not destroy so much good equipment.'

Lois was still standing. Her voice rose almost to a scream.

'What do you want? Why are you doing it? We haven't harmed you. Haven't you had enough war? Don't you know what it did to Earth?'

'It is rather late to discuss large issues,' said Byelinsky. 'However, I think history has proven that two wholly different ways of thought cannot long co-exist. Sooner or later, one will begin to dominate the other, which then has no choice but violence. The Khanate has adopted a radically different solution from yours to the problems facing us all. It is a way which will seem hard to most. They will naturally tend to follow the softer, easier, half-hearted way of the west. But since that is no solution at all, but merely means ruin in the end, it must go.'

A muscle jumped in the angle of O'Neill's jaw. 'It seems I've heard that song before,' he muttered. 'Just what do you Siberians propose to do?'

'Face the facts,' answered Byelinsky. 'Acknowledge that man's whole evolution has taken a new course. It is not a course that I, personally, am very happy about. I agree that the last war was suicidal stupidity, and that the issues it was fought over mean nothing when there are no men left. Nevertheless, it is now true that man's heredity is, on the whole, ruined, and that there is no chance of restoring the old norm. Therefore, if intelligent life is to survive at all, it must be protected. It must not be allowed to lose what few good genes, even improved genes, that are left, in a great sea of malformed types. You made a feeble attempt in that direction yourselves, but under your social system it just will not work. Another approach – regrettably, a forcible one – must be tried.'

'In other words,' said O'Neill slowly, 'what you're doing is setting up the old master-slave system. A little clique of aristocrats and a big mass of degraded serfs.'

'Those are emotional words,' said Byelinsky. 'The best solution for man at large seems to be his controlled evolution into specialized species. Naturally, such a system cannot be democratic, which is admittedly a shame.' He looked out into the Martian darkness, and for a minute his face was strangely bitter. 'I recall how it once was, before the war. Do you not think I would trade my life to have that back? But it cannot be.' Turning to them, briskly: 'The importance of Mars as a place for colonization and research is fully recognized by the Khan. Since we are convinced that your view of the problem is misguided and can only lead to disaster for the entire race, we do not intend that you shall have this planet.

'A single military base here, equipped for aerial attack, could hold Mars against all comers – interplanetary logistics being what it is. Naturally, America will not know that we are here, and will not know what is destroying her ships. Our best socio-economic mathematicians estimate that two more such attempts at most will be made, thereafter Mars will be given up and the moon used as an alternative. One which is, of course, not nearly so satisfactory, in spite of being closer.'

'Look,' said Lois, with a hopeless kind of pleading in her voice, 'you're being blind. We know the facts as well as you do. Our idea is to learn more facts, though. Learn enough genetics to change things.'

Byelinsky smiled, a curiously sad smile. 'Believe me, the Khanate scientists considered that approach carefully,' he replied. 'It was felt that the probability of success is too low to justify the enormous cost in time, materials, labor, and intellectual effort. For the same investment, we could be *certain* of large results in our own more modest plan. And mankind is one, you know; national sovereignty is an insane myth. We will not long permit other states to waste resources belonging to all humanity on visionary schemes.'

'If we try, and fail,' said O'Neill, 'we'll still have remained free. What's the use of the race surviving, if it's going to be in an anthill society where even the masters are slaves?'

'You see,' said Byelinsky. 'I told you we could not argue basic philosophy. You and I will never agree, because at bottom it is an emotional and not a rational question.' He shook his head. 'But to my mind, there is something healthy about a will to survive at all costs, and something wrong about your clinging to abstract symbols which will have no meaning if man becomes extinct.'

Ivanovitch raised his shaggy head and asked a question in Russian. Byelinsky answered in English: 'As for what will happen to you, I repeat that you need have no fear as long as you behave yourselves – or at least refrain from misbehaving too badly. You will be well treated, and when we get back to Siberia you will be received with honor.'

'As breedin' stock!' snapped Collie.

'Why, yes.' Byelinsky grinned. 'And just what is your objection to that?' He got up when they had been quiet for a while. 'I will bid you goodnight, then,' he said. 'If you have any needs or desires, do not hesitate to ask your guards. They all speak Russian, at least.'

Down the ladder, then, and through a hall and a couple of rooms where bunks were crowded close together. Near the waist of the ship, a door was opened by the Oriental, who bowed them through. It clanged behind them with a terribly final note.

Lois looked around her, and slow amazement grew in her eyes. 'Why –' she breathed at last. 'Why, it's like a – suite!'

'It is one,' grunted O'Neill. 'Saints, this is better quarters than they give their crew.' He cocked one eyebrow. 'It looks as if their main idea in coming to Mars was to capture us alive. Which suggests that if we cooperate, we can become privileged characters in Siberia.'

'Yeah,' muttered Collie. 'Reckon we can.'

There were four small rooms and a tiny bath, but after their own ship the space and fittings were overwhelming. Light folding bunks, tables and chairs, indirect illumination, even rugs on the floor. Collie noticed a microviewer and a good collection of film books in English, and when he opened a drawer there were some games. Inside a closet hung the unbelievable luxury of clean clothes. The door leading out, he found, was now locked, but a shutter opening from the inside covered a grille. Looking through this, he noticed a guard, who came over and stood courteously waiting. Collie closed the shutter in his face.

'Well,' said Ivanovitch heavily, 'w'y not use de t'ings? Lois, you want de first bat'?'

She nodded and took a dress from the closet and went into the cubicle. A squeal of delight came through the door: 'It's got a shower!'

'How the deuce can they afford the water?' asked Collie.

'Oh, that can be recovered easily enough,' said O'Neill. He took a restless turn about the room. 'But still, this gilt-edged cattle pen takes plenty of room and weight. You know, even with two ships, and even without having brought as much machinery and stuff as we, I doubt if the Siberian force can be more than fifteen men as of now. They must plan on leaving some here, in our installations.' His lean face tightened, and he drove one fist into his open palm. 'By all the saints! Collie, Misha, if we could get away, get word to Captain Wayne of just how the situation is – I believe *we* could take over!'

'Yeah, sure,' said Collie, 'Get away – how?'

'That I don't know,' said O'Neill roughly. 'But we've got to. One of us, at least.' He looked at the others. They had stretched out on bunks and their muscles were loose with weariness. 'Unless.' he said, very slowly, 'you don't want to. I imagine a stud in Siberia would live pretty well, at that.'

'We'll talk about it tomorrow,' said Collie, turning his eyes from the gaunt fanatic face. He didn't want to argue now. He didn't even want to think about it. He just wanted to wash up and turn in and sleep for a week.

14

A guard brought in breakfast while another stood by to cover him. The food was ordinary space rations, but at least it was hot, and Collie devoured his share blissfully. He still felt the drowsy remoteness of a long night's sleep and the ending of tension within him, and when the guards were gone he blinked amiably at O'Neill's restless prowling. Ivanovitch had gone back to bed and was snoring thunderously; Lois sat quietly on the edge of her bunk and watched the Irishman as he paced.

'Hell take it!' O'Neill swung around finally to glare at Collie. 'We've got to escape. We've got to get word back to our ship.'

'Uh, yeah, but how?' The hillman yawned and stretched himself. 'Look, Tom, we're here in a shipful of armed men. We'd have to hike across the desert, which means an airsuit. Not just any suit, but our own pers'nal ones, tailored to fit our pers'nal bodies. You tell me how we do all this.'

'Given up, have you – already?'

'N-n-no-o-o. Just tryin' to use my head a little.' Collie

wondered if he really meant it.

'*You* wouldn't mind sleeping with a hundred women assigned to you,' said O'Neill harshly. 'But Lois –'

The girl looked away. 'Don't, Tom,' she said.

Collie bit his lip. He hadn't thought of that angle. Yeah – it would be different for a woman. Unless – 'Mebbe they can grow kids in tanks,' he ventured. 'I've heard talk about that.'

'Ectogenesis . . . yes, I suppose it could be developed.' O'Neill threw himself into a chair. 'What of it? Don't you care who you work for?'

Collie paused, feeling for an answer. He wondered if he did. Sure, the Siberian society was not very attractive, but it would have its privileged members, especially in the first few generations, and he could probably be one of them. And he would be on Earth, Earth the green, Earth the fair, Earth of tall skies and summer nights and autumn leaves and the small sweet rain. He would be home.

The girl shook her head, light sliding along the bronze of her hair. Looking over to her, he saw in her eyes the struggle with horror.

Collie opened his mouth. 'Tom –'

'Yes?' O'Neill leaped nervously up. 'What is it?'

Collie brought himself up hard and sat for a moment shaking. How could they have forgotten? It would be strange if their prison didn't hold some microphonic listener.

'Never mind,' he said. Then, after a moment: 'No, it won't work, Tom. This is one jail that's too good to break out of.' *Don't overdo it*, he cautioned himself. 'Mebbe back on Earth we'll have our chance, but not here.'

'But here will be our last chance!'

Collie got up and walked over to him. 'All right, think up some bright scheme,' he said irritably, 'but don't bother me with it till you've got one.' He rummaged through the desk. 'I'd like to play some bridge, if we can wake Misha up. Got anything to keep score on?'

'No,' said Lois. She was watching him with sudden intentness. 'No writing materials. I checked that.'

'Too bad. How 'bout some checkers, then, Tom?' Collie took the Irishman's hand. For a moment O'Neill looked as if he were going to snatch it back. Collie's finger traced in the palm: *W*. O'Neill stared. Collie made an *A*. Suddenly O'Neill nodded.

Collie went on: *T-C-H* (pause) *O-U-T* (pause) *T-H-E-Y* (pause) *M-A-Y* (pause) *B-E* (pause) *L-I-S-T-E-N-I-N-G*.

'Sure,' said O'Neill. His voice wobbled, just a bit. 'Sure, I'll take you on.'

'I'll kibitz, if you don't mind.' Lois strolled over to them. Collie thought how graceful she was.

'No talkin', then,' he said. 'This is serious business.'

He got out the board and set it up like a half-played game, just in case. Then the three of them sat down to writing. The table top made a fair surface, and speed grew with practice. Now and then Collie missed a letter, but he found that on the whole he could follow the successive shapes if they were large enough.

Collie: Okay. I'm on your side. But just how do we get loose?

O'Neill: You're right about our having to have our own suits. Let's plan on that basis.

Lois: If we could overpower a guard and make him take us to the airlock.

O'Neill: No. They need only use tear gas on us.

They worried the problem for slow hours. Now and then they talked aloud, just to prevent suspicion. The scheme was not born in a flash, it was hammered out with trouble and argument, and in the end there were many misgivings about it. Informing Ivanovitch was a hurdle in itself, he was hardly able to follow the invisible writing and Collie felt wet and weak by the time the giant understood.

Then it was but to await the chance.

Lunch was over and they were dealing out a half-hearted game of rummy when there was a knock on the door. O'Neill sprang up, spilling the cards, and his voice was high and strained: 'Come in.'

'Easy, Tom,' whispered Lois, pulling him down. 'Keep your mouth shut. You'll give the show away.'

The lock clicked and the door opened. Byelinsky stood there in front of an armed guard, smiling. 'I wondered how you were,' he said. 'Is there anything you need?'

'Um-m-m – Well –' Collie rubbed his chin, not daring to look into the crinkled blue eyes. 'No, I reckon not. We're fairly well off.'

'You could –' Lois moistened her lips. 'You could tell us about – the whole situation. Our friends, for instance, what you plan to do with them.'

'I told you, we desire to capture them alive, though not with any further loss to ourselves.' The colonel sat down on a bunk, crossing thick-muscled legs. 'An expedition is being readied. Unless they are fools, they will yield without anyone's being hurt.'

'An' what then?' asked Collie. 'Where do we go from here?'

'Well, some further developmental work must be done on your camp,' said the Siberian. 'We plan to leave a few men here, to continue the job until our next ship arrives. But you personally can expect to leave for Earth within two months.'

'So you put us in a cell there,' blurted O'Neill. 'What have we to look forward to?'

'Oh, be reasonable,' snapped Byelinsky. 'There is a gigantic work to be done. You, as favorable mutants, can pick your own jobs, within broad limits. If you keep yourselves politically clean, you can expect to prosper.'

'Okay, okay,' said Collie. 'Ain't no arguin' with you, like the sheep said to the catamount.'

Byelinsky chuckled. 'I would like to see you as content as possible,' he said after a moment. 'If you wish anything we can safely give you, just tell us.'

'Well –' Inside, Collie's muscles tautened. He felt that it must blaze from him, that the enemy could not help but see. The thoughts that roared in his head, they must hear them, how could he ever – His voice sounded very remote, the voice of someone else: 'Well, come to think of it, there is one little thing.'

'Yes?'

'Let us go outside for a bit, just to walk around, huh? We're all used to exercisin' a lot, every day. It ain't easy just to sit here in a narrow space like this.'

'Please, Mr. Collingwood.' Byelinsky raised his hand. 'I wish you wouldn't take me for such a complete fool.'

'Suit yourself.' Collie shrugged. 'If you're that scared of us, I s'pose we'd better stay in here.'

'It is a matter of assigning guards,' said Byelinsky defensively.

'Our men have their own work to do, you know.'

It was no part of the plan, but: 'Oh, hell,' said Collie, 'hobble us, put us on ropes, do whatever you want, but let us stretch our legs a little.'

'Hm. Very well, then.' Byelinsky gave an order in Russian. Turning back to his prisoners: 'I think we can let you have about an hour a day outside.'

'Okay.' The effort of keeping his voice casual seemed to drain Collie. He didn't dare look at the others. 'Thanks.'

'Have a good time,' said Byelinsky mildly. He got up and went out again. The door closed behind him.

O'Neill bent over the table and began tracing letters: What do you think we will do?

Collie: Don't know. But maybe we'll be able to make a break.

Lois: It will have to be you. You are the only one who would stand a chance.

Collie: Yes. Don't risk your own life, Lois. I want to come back to you.

She looked away. Shyly, he bent over and kissed her. She sighed and walked over to her bunk and sat down.

The door opened again. Four guards in airsuits stood there. One laid down their own Mars-equipment.

As he changed into his reeking undergarment, Collie glanced at his airsuit. Only one oxy tank. Byelinsky wasn't taking any chances. No man could get within range of the American power-beam on one tank if he had to move fast. Even on two.

No *man*.

Collie shivered as he dragged the heavy fabric over his body. With the casual care of long practice, he checked the units: pump, batteries, heating coils. Yes, it was all there, all working, though he couldn't be sure if the batteries were fully charged. But no water, no sun-cell, no compass, no –

They shuffled slowly down the metal ways. The dark Martian sky yawned before them when the outer airlock door opened. Descending the ladder, Collie studied the layout. Men were working over in one end of the camp, setting up a light mobile cannon. That must be for the attack. A group of soldiers could haul the gun, as well as a wagon full of ammunition and supplies.

One well-placed shell would break the rocket motor of the ship, and after that its crew would be helpless.

He felt hard gritty earth under his feet, and stood waiting for the others. A rifle pointed unmovingly at his midriff. His eyes shifted, considering the terrain. To the north, the scored hills fell sharply into the ravine. That was the way he'd have to go.

'Come on,' said O'Neill. The thin vicious sun-blaze hid his face behind the helmet, and the sound-amplifiers strained expression from his voice. Thanks be for that. The Irishman was no actor. 'Round and round and round we go.'

They strode in a circle about the ships, once, twice, three times, with the guards accompanying them a few yards off. Imperceptibly, Collie widened the radius as much as he dared. Sweat was cold along his spine, under his arms, on his palms. Three minutes from now, he thought, he might be a sprawled corpse.

There had been no way of knowing what arrangement would be made for guarding. They had to improvise. But Ivanovitch's strength would be necessary. The Russian edged around until he was on Collie's right, between his comrades and the ship.

Around and around and around.

Now the north end of the camp swinging back, the ships behind him, the working party on their far side, the guards – perhaps – just a trifle relaxed . . . Desperately, Collie wished he could wait, go through this routine every day for a week until suspicion was eased. But there wasn't time, there wasn't time. In a week, the Americans would be overwhelmed. He gathered himself.

'*Go!*'

No time for fear, then. He made one giant bound that brought him against the guard on his left. One hand batted the rifle aside, the other grabbed and tried to wrest it loose. His foot slammed a mule-kick to the belly.

The man went down, choking. Collie fell on top of him as the bullets spanged overhead. Then O'Neill was on one guard and Ivanovitch was tangling with the other two.

The man under Collie struggled, nearly throwing him off. Collie got an armlock and heaved. He felt bone snap. Then he had the rifle. He twisted it around and shot point-blank into the Siberian's helmet.

He could hear slugs whining, he seemed to be in a rain of them. It was no time to help the others. He turned the body around on its back. Blood was running through the smashed helmet, steaming as it hit the ground. Collie wrenched the man's oxygen tank out of its clamps. It took both his arms to carry it, he couldn't have the rifle. He got up and ran.

Now if Misha could hold them off long enough – and not get himself killed doing it, the big brave fool –

O'Neill was still down, wrestling with his guard, but held where he was. Lois huddled into the sand, there was nothing she could do but hide from the bullets. Ivanovitch had gotten a tommy-gun away from one man and turned it on him.

The Russian felt a blow that brought whirling darkness. He lurched in his tracks, dropped to one knee, and gave the remaining guard a burst. The working party was coming around the ships. Ivanovitch crouched where he was and fired at them.

There was no pain. There was a huge numbness where he had been hit, and he seemed strangely light. *Like being drunk*, he thought. The approaching soldiers seemed to double themselves and become one again, they seemed to waver and ripple. It was like looking at them through water, through the cool green water of Earth.

He saw himself. Blood and smoking air, his suit was torn open by the gunfire burst and so was he. Nobody else could have kept going this long. His heart clamored in his breast, but he still felt as if he himself were very far away, happily drunk back on Earth. He knelt in the Martian sand and fired.

Got to hold them off, got to let Collie get away, can't remember why butitdoesntmatterwhygottodoit.

There is a giant buzzing now, as of many bees, there are bees humming drowsily through a wild field of clover, all the world is drunk with summer. Lie down in the clover, under a tree that is full of wind and sunlight, lie down and drink the smell of clover through your nostrils, and a million million honeybees zum zum zum. Oh, there are horses running in the field, sunlight flows like cool water off their flanks, there is the good clean smell of horses.

Let me rest my head in thy lap, O woman, let thy hair flow over me, it is a tent of summer, I can see Earth's sky through the strands of thy hair, let me sleep for a little while, for I have drunk deep and now it is growing dark. Soon there will be stars.

15

Behind an ocherous bluff, Collie stopped and fumbled awkwardly till he felt the stolen oxy tank slip into its rack. Now he had two of them. He turned down the valve of the one he was using, letting his pump suck in Martian air as a supplement. And the heating coils could also be kept low, because he'd be working up a sweat.

He turned then, and began to run. The crack and stutter of gunfire faded swiftly behind him, but he couldn't tell if the fight was over yet. As long as Misha could keep shooting, there would be no pursuit, but that battle wouldn't last much longer. *Christ, I hope he comes through. I told him again and again not to take risks but –*

He forgot Ivanovitch and O'Neill in the rising worry about Lois. What if a bullet caught her, opened her suit and threw her down into the sand coughing blood? If she died, if they had to close her eyes, there would be no reason to keep going, no reason why he should not sink into Martian dust himself. *I love that girl,* he thought. It was the first time he had fully acknowledged the fact.

He dismissed his own personality. Now he was just a running machine.

He burst from a long pebbly draw and came out on the high, rolling desert. Stealing a glance behind, he could not see the ships in the valley, but he was still less than a mile from them. Bullets would carry far on Mars. He wanted to make a wild dash, but that was no way to cover long distances. Easy does it, loping strides, feel the yards and the miles slip away underfoot.

He'd have to circle around. There was at least one runner his equal among the Siberians, who could hound him down on the straightaway. He had to shake their pursuit first, and then come back to his goal, and hope he didn't get lost in the process. It would be a dreadful thing to get lost on Mars.

The pounding jar of his footfalls shocked into him. His heart was already beginning to beat heavily, his lungs felt dry, he wasn't getting enough air. Reluctantly, he turned up his oxygen valve a little.

His air pump whined to a halt. He drew a deep breath to hold him while he opened the oxy valve fully. Someone had finally thought to turn off the power-beam to his suit. He wondered how long a tank would last.

Well, he thought grimly, *I'll soon find out.*

Another look behind – yes, he could see small figures climbing over the valley ridge. They could see him, too, and his trail in the sand. He forced himself to continue at a steady pace.

But he had to break the trail. Up ahead there, a jumbled mass of boulders. They looked closer than they were, in this clear air. He swore to himself, damn it, were they running from him as he neared? His feet thudded softly over the ground, kicking up little spurts of dust that were slow to settle.

The rocks seemed to rise above him all at once. He sprang up on the nearest. Another glance behind – the Siberians had lost ground, they couldn't keep up with him, but with their extra air supplies they could run him down over a long stretch.

If they can find me! He went soaring from boulder to boulder. Dropping into a gash between two of them, he wormed rapidly to one side, slithered across another rock, and ran low-crouching at an angle down the stony ridge. His overtaxed heart seemed to shake his whole body.

The heap of boulders came to an abrupt end, and the revealing sand stretched beyond them to the horizon. He paused, gasping. Yes, over that way, a little patch of woods. He jumped from the last rock into the growth and went carefully through it for a mile or so, trying not to leave marks of his passage. At its end he stopped for a breather and a look behind. Nothing else, no movement, only the sand and the quietness. It seemed to shimmer and wobble around him. A trick of his eyes?

Well, he thought, he must have come a good two or three miles all told without leaving any traces – he hoped. Now he could bend down to some straightforward running. He got his direction from the sun and began his trek.

The sand rolled away under his feet. He ran for the horizon, but it was always just as far. There was a dreadful sameness to this part of the desert, it would be all too easy to get lost. If he did, they might dig him up a thousand years from now and wonder who he had been.

Thirst began to nag him. He tried to ignore the need. There was no water. There was only the sand, and the sky, and the running.

Nobody else, he thought, could even have attempted this marathon. He was relying on his own mutant strengths, the powerful legs and the deep lungs and the air-hoarding blood. But he wondered if they would be enough.

In and out, in and out, in and out. He grew aware of the stiffness of his suit. It resisted his movements, not much, but enough so he could notice it. The joints must need oiling. It might be the one small factor which would kill him.

Something skittered from his path, a tiny animal, desert-colored. It was scared and he was scared and his enemies were scared – a whole cosmos full of fear. He ran on.

The sun slipped westward. He had to stop for a while, his spleen was beginning to hurt him too much. Twisting his neck, he got a look at the gauge on the oxy tank he was using. Pretty near empty. He didn't sit down, but walked slowly ahead, trying to keep stiffness from his muscles.

It seemed unbelievable that he should be here, caught in this fantastic thing, running across another world against death. Such things didn't happen to him. They happened to somebody else. It was always somebody else who ran, and fell, and lay there till he died. For the first time, he had the full chilling awareness of his own mortality.

Sundown. He got speed on again. The stars burned and blazed overhead. He didn't recognize most of the constellations, they were the same as on Earth but this was a different latitude. He wished he could see the Great Bear or wintry Orion. It was utterly still, his feet rang loudly on iron-hard ground, the stars glittered enormously quiet. How high they were! The sky seemed infinitely deep and black. It seemed forever since he had walked out with Lois under those high bright suns.

The cold began to strike in at him. He shivered, but even his running could not keep him warm. To a being with infrared vision, he must have flamed like a torch in that frozen landscape. He turned up his heater a little. The vapors of his body were chokingly thick now, fogging his helmet. If he'd had a dew-bottle along, he could have breathed out into that, trapped the water and drunk it. God, but he needed a drink! As it was, he had to open his valve and let out a puff of air. It rose white, like a small ghost, and disappeared. He was drying out piece by piece, withering by installments.

No more air. His heart ran wild, and he felt the involuntary panic of it. Hastily, he discarded the one tank and plugged his air hose into the other. He allowed himself the luxury of a long breath before turning down the valve. It was stinging and heady, a clean smell of metal in his nose.

He was among hills again, low but rugged, steep sides hiding their treacheries in night. If a sharp rock snagged his suit open, well – He took another glance at the stars. The ship ought to be that way. But it would be so easy to miss it by a few miles, pass just over the horizon and go stumbling in the sand till he died.

Even if he was on the right bearing, he wasn't sure he'd make it. At the rate he was consuming air, his other tank probably wouldn't last long enough. He slowed his pace as much as he dared, trotting over stones that rattled and sand that gritted. But he couldn't go too slow. There was the enemy, who might find his trail; and a section of them would surely try to strike directly at the American camp before he could arrive with his warning; and there was thirst, and airlessness, and cold.

On and on. The loneliness was overwhelming. He might have been the last man on a dead and ruined world. The stones underfoot might have been skulls. He was beginning to feel dizzy now, more and more of his mind was dropping off into sleep. He cursed and tried to flog his energies up again. If he lost his wits, then he was done for.

Pursuit, distance, cold, thirst, suffocation. Add one more enemy to the list: himself.

How far had he come? There was no telling. He tried to count his steps, but he lost track. He stumbled on something, and went down on his stomach, and lay there sobbing.

Up, for God's sake! The stiffness clawed at him. He wanted to lie there and rest, he wanted to drown himself in water. There was an ocean in him, lapping under the surface of his mind, there was a warm primeval ocean, he thought he could hear a lulling wind blow across it, he thought he could sink down into its darkness and find sleep.

He grew aware of the noise in his head, long thunderous waves, flashes like sunlight running along their foam. The stars began to flow together, constellations snake-danced before his eyes, he wanted to cry but he was too withered.

Oxygen lack – He turned the valve wide open and sucked air into his lungs. For a moment, he almost passed out. Maybe he did. The stars steadied, hard and bright and merciless. He could see clear to the horizon, where it cut off the Milky Way.

His feet were like someone else's now, they moved without his own will. The brief clarity vanished again. There was just enough of his consciousness left to watch the stars and gauge his direction. He didn't care any longer whether he made it or not.

Brightness in the east, growing and climbing, the shrunken sun ablaze on the rim of the world. Had he been going so long?

He was plodding now, bent over, his arms swinging stiffly. Once, jerking toward awareness, he realized that his swollen tongue was hanging out between his teeth, and pulled it back in again. The sand dunes seemed to ripple, there was a restless shimmer on the desert as if he waded through water. Once more he thought he could hear the remote rushing of waves.

The gauge said empty. He turned on his air pump, drawing power from the batteries, and tossed the cylinder into the dust. It was a niggard breath the pump gave him, and its dryness was like a flame in his mouth and nose and throat. He tried to lope, but fell to the ground, and lay there for a long while before he had the strength to get up. After that he walked.

And walked.

The sun was a blind dazzle overhead. He didn't bother checking his direction any more. He slogged with his face turned toward the ground, his eyes closed most of the time. Once in a while he would look up, but there was only the desert.

No – wait – many centuries later, he saw the hard flash of metal. It was the ship. He knew dully that he had found his way home, but he couldn't remember why he had come.

The air pump sighed and sputtered. *Low voltage*, he thought, without knowing what the words meant. *Batteries about done for*. He looked ahead at the ship. It didn't seem any closer. Nobody was around. Should there have been? he asked himself vaguely.

His feet rose and fell, rose and fell, rose and fell. You pick 'em up and lay 'em down, you pick 'em up and lay 'em down, you pick 'em up and lay 'em down, you . . .

The pump whined to a halt. He didn't feel the cold that bit through his suit. The ship disappeared in ragged blacknesses. He kept on walking.

Then the blacknesses ran together, and rose up and hit him in the face, and he fell down into the great waiting ocean.

16

The hook bites back and claws itself fast. For a moment you jerk, in the utter astonishment of pain and awareness, down in a lightless dream. Then you feel the line drawing you upward.

Sunlight burns in a watery sky. Almost, you can see the monstrous shape of the Fisher, but your brain is a dimness with only the red hook-slash to give it color. And you know, blindly and horribly, that the Fisher will drag you up into the sunlight.

You clamp on the leader and pull away, rushing down again toward the bottom of the sea. Your head slams around, your whole body, at the savage jerk of the line. You thresh about, bending yourself into an arc, biting fins and tail into the cool soft water and the darkness. The line is drawn wire-taut, and your whole being is one great No.

Up, then, tugging and yanking and fighting aware only of the hook and the hard light, wishing only the sea depths. From a million miles away, the Fisher speaks, and his voice booms and echoes through the hollow cosmos. Crazily, you fight, and break the surface. The dry sharp air is a knife in your gills, the light is a hot roaring fire in your eyes. The voice of the Fisher resounds between a million watching stars.

'*He's coming around.*'

Cycles of time wheel and thunder as you come around, biting your own tail in the pain of it. The line slackens, ever so faintly, and you plunge down again for the dear darkness. O spawn of night and primeval wetness, hurled gasping into the air, the hook is a living thing in your mouth, you spew out your own guts but the hook is still there. And the line is drawing, and you rise again into the terrible sky.

The Fisher has you now, there is only the pain and whirling whirling whirling, strengthless you lie back against the line and are drawn ashore. For a moment, then, you flutter in mud, and the ocean drains from you, great waters rush down, cataracting over brain and nerve and bone, to lie still and waiting at the bottom of your skull. The ocean will wait for you, down in darkness.

And you lie without power in a slowly tearing night, and look up into the face of the Fisher.

'Are you all right, Collie?' Alaric Wayne's voice was very soft, gentle as a woman's hand.

'Y-y-yeah.' He looked about him. His head weighed enormously, it was all he could do to turn it on the pillow, but there was a curious light clarity in him. His thoughts seemed to have winged feet, skimming over the surface of a mind washed clean by some long rain. 'I – made it?'

'Damn near didn't,' grunted Feinberg. 'You conked out a couple of miles from the ship. If we hadn't been watching for anything – we wouldn't 'a seen you. Damn near dead when we brought you in.'

'I – I – s-s-sorry we had to be so rough w-w-with you,' faltered Wayne. 'Plasma, drugs, we *had* to wake you up as fast as possible without killing you.'

'Yeah, reckon so.' Collie was whispering, but the ship was so quiet that they had no trouble hearing. 'Kind of urgent.'

'What happened?' snapped Arakelian. 'What's the story?'

It seemed a curiously distant adventure, as if it had happened to someone else. He told it in a few words.

At the end, they nodded bleakly. 'All right,' said Feinberg. 'I guess you can rest now. You deserve it.'

Collie lay without other movement than his breathing, looking empty-minded up at the ceiling. It felt good. Drowsy and good.

Presently the pain started, he grew aware of just how parched and burned his membranes were, just how sore his muscles felt. He could barely lift a hand to the water jug beside him. He lay drinking through the zero-gravity tube, *like a baby*, he thought with weak amusement, but the water didn't help much. Still, he could feel strength returning, minute by minute he got back more of his control.

Feinberg came in. 'How're you doing, boy?'

'Okay, I reckon,' said Collie.

'There's no damage done,' said Feinberg. 'You've got some frostbites, and of course there's the effects of extreme thirst and some anoxia, but you'll be as good as new in a week.'

'If we live another week.'

'Good point there. Our jolly friends with the cannon ought to be along pretty soon, and we've only got short-range defenses. We're trying to figure out what to do.'

'Well, how 'bout lettin' me sit in on it?'

'If you feel strong enough. You should be able to give some useful advice. Tell you what, I'll bring you some soup, and after that we'll all confer here in the bunkroom. Got to mount a couple of lookouts, but they can talk over the intercom.'

Half an hour later, Feinberg and Wayne came to sit by Collie's bunk; Gammony and Arakelian were on guard duty elsewhere in the ship. Faces were drawn taut by strain. Collie realized that it had not been an easy time for those who stayed behind.

'If they knew who you were,' said Arakelian over the intercom, 'their spies must really have cased us before we left Earth. They came loaded for bear.'

'So far,' said Feinberg, 'we've only hit one really practical course of action. That's to scram out of here and back to Earth.'

'But Lois – Misha an' Tom –' protested Collie. 'If they're still alive.'

'You don't think any of us like the notion, do you?' Feinberg scowled. 'Still, if we try to play Quixote we may not even be able to warn people at home. There are five of us left, counting you who're on the sick list. We got a couple of rifles and a Wayne resonator which is only effective at sixty feet or less. What the hell have we got to fight with?'

The captain nodded. It was strange how he looked, more like a child which had been hurt than the chief of a mission. His voice was very low. 'I cannot see any other solution. If we had some sort of aircraft – but we do not.'

'We got the spaceship,' said Gammony over the intercom.

'And you, of all people, know how little maneuverable she is,' said Arakelian. 'Straight up or straight down, that's really all she's good for in a gravity field.'

'Hey –' Collie sat up. His abused muscles drew him back with a groan. 'Hey, they ain't got any air defense. We could bring the ship right down on top o' theirs. Fry 'em with our blast!'

'By God! No.' Feinberg shook his head. 'Unless we want to fry our own people too.'

'Yeah. I forgot about that.' Collie grimaced.

'Though wait –' Wayne's mouth drew into a thin line. 'It may be the best course. Sacrificing three lives, yes, but still there are large issues.' He looked at the floor, clasping and unclasping his hands. 'Forgive me,' he mumbled.

'Ah'm not so shore we could do it, anyways,' said Gammony. 'This heah boat's tricky. We'd prob'ly have to come down so slow, from so high above, they'd have plenty time to get out from under.'

'If we had a heavy gun –' breathed Arakelian. 'We could land right in their camp, maybe. They'd have to yield.'

'I dunno,' said Collie. 'That colonel o' theirs is a tough man!'

'All right, so we hole them. Air doesn't puff out right away, you know, if there's only one hole. They'll have time to get on suits, and so will our friends.' Arakelian chuckled without humor. 'It's a side issue, though. We haven't got a heavy gun.'

'Wait . . . wait . . .' Alaric Wayne sprang to his feet. There was a sudden blaze in his pale eyes. '*Don't we?*'

They looked at the slim figure, there was a descending silence, and he knew they were expecting Wayne the superman, Wayne the unconquerable, Wayne the magician, to pull a rabbit from the hat. It drove him into stuttering, for a while he could only gibber at them. He knew his face was writhing and his body in a tremble, and he wanted to run and hide, but there was no place to go.

'I think I get it,' said Feinberg slowly.

Gammony spoke, they could almost see him shaking his head. 'Hoo, man, y'all shore 'spect a lot o' this-heah boat, don' yo'?'

17

In the following dawn, Collie was woken up. He leaned on Arakelian and made a painful way to the bridge. Today he would be needed, or he would be dead. It wasn't a bad choice, as such things went.

Feinberg was in the engine room, Gammony and Arakelian strapped themselves into the pilot chairs, Collie was given a seat near the main viewport. Wayne sat next to his dog, with a thing in his lap that was small and ugly, a hastily assembled confusion of tubes and coils and meters, with a cable running back to the main power-line. It seemed incredible that this could be the weapon which was their hope.

The motors began to talk, warming up, and their voice shook in the hull and rattled teeth together and filled the heart with a sudden meaningless clutch of terror. *Subsonics*, Collie told himself, and tried to ignore the fear; but it rode with him. When he looked outside the landscape seemed wholly sinister. There it was, the desert, sand and dust and gaunt gray needles, streaked with mineral veins, curving toward a dark bloodless hue, the color of death. And yet, he thought, with a lifting within him, this haggard world was the future. It was bare and cold and cruel, but even in its darkest night there were more stars than you saw from Earth.

Someday, he thought, it would be green out there.

There were human voices now, become flat and impersonal and machine-like. 'Number One bank ready. Number Two bank ready, Number Three bank ready . . .' Fingers were dancing over the control panel, weaving in and out between flashing lights, an oddly beautiful thing to watch. Gammony's head was cocked to one side, his eyes half-closed, as he blent his senses with those of the ship. 'Five seconds, four seconds, three seconds . . .'

The rocket lifted on a tail of fire, *br-r-room, br-r-room, br-r-room,* and Collie saw the landscape fall down and there was only the sky to be seen. They were moving at two Mars gravities, one emgee effective, it was extravagant of fuel but they had to swing that huge mass through heaven as slowly as it would go. If they won out, they could get enough fuel from the Siberian craft. Or could they? Collie wouldn't put it past Byelinsky to blow up the whole world. He thought of living here on Mars, eking out rations, making pitiful attempts to grow some food, starving and dying and cursing the sky which sent no relief.

Thunder in the ship, thunder in the skull. From where he sat, Collie could see the big chart of Mars, on which he had marked the Siberian camp. He could not read the radar screen on which they located their own position, but Arakelian's eyes were flickering over it, never resting, and his hands danced with Gammony's. *Pas de deux* in a ballet called *Man's Hope*. Or was it *Man's Dying*?

Gammony nodded, ever so slightly, and spoke something into the throat microphone which linked him with Arakelian and Feinberg. Three men, three parts of one ponderous machine, three little bundles of spongy gray tissue which had dreamed the machine into being. Slowly, the spaceship began to tilt forward.

This was the maneuver they would have thought impossible even a day ago, which might still be impossible. The ship was a thing of free space, a whale meant to swim in currents of gravitational force, she could no more be jockeyed over a planetary surface than a fish could walk on land. Trying to fly her was an insanity. She would tilt too far and crash a mile down into the desert, she would split open under the stream and scatter herself across half Mars, she would crack a seam and whiff her air out and choke the crew where they sat. And yet, it had to be done. They could not go up into clear space, orbit around, and descend on the enemy camp, it would take too long and be too inaccurate. They had to do the impossible, or smash themselves into the face of Mars.

After all, there *is* a fish which can cross dry land.

Collie stole a look around. The pilots were lost to humanness, they had merged themselves utterly with the ship – Gammony's balance and Arakelian's speed and Feinberg's delicate touch holding her teetering on the edge of ruin. (Thus far and no farther, or she'll heel over and nosedive . . . Slap that button! . . . So, girl, so, steady, easy does it . . .)

Wayne sat relaxed, there was peace in his eyes. This was something he could understand, the huge interplay of mass and force, the

167

simple realities of living and dying. The dog huddled close to him, his sullenness become a gentle trust.

It struck Collie afresh how this conquest was something new to history. It would not be done by blood and iron and cunning, in spite of their present mission. It was a matter of patience, knowledge, slow building and planning and waiting. The enemy was not, ultimately, other men, it was a universe never really meant for humanity, and you had conquered it when you understood it.

The thunder brawled around him. Once he saw Wayne smile across the narrow space and indicate a set of ragged pips on the radar. His lips formed words: 'Siberian party.' Yes, it would be Byelinsky's men, trundling their ridiculous gun across desolation. They would be gaping upward in total bewilderment, and then, no doubt, they would wheel around and begin the heartbreaking struggle back to their camp. But when they got there, the issue would already be decided – one way or another.

Collie tried to push fear out of himself, and looked at the sky. It was a deep midnight blue overhead, a serene and lovely color. Mars wasn't such a bad world, taking it all in all. If he had Lois with him, he could well imagine returning here and settling down and growing up with the colony. The happy man was he who had given his life to something big.

Once the ship tilted horribly. Collie's head spun and he grabbed the chair arms with a stark knowledge that now he was going to die. But she fought herself back, roaring and stuttering, she moved clumsily through heaven again.

And now, now, now they were descending, splashing fire as they came down, now was the moment of decision.

Collie saw the tall forms of the Siberian vessels lift into view, he saw the remembered hills and the pathetic little lost cluster of machines and crates. They must have burst so suddenly into sight, with such devastating unexpectedness, that there had been no time for the enemy to blast off. It took so long to warm up a motor that he was locked here and could only wait – unless he had some unknown weapon in reserve.

The rockets cut out, the ship shuddered once and then was wholly quiet. Gammony and Arakelian slumped in their chairs, sweat-soaked and shaking. They had landed.

No movement around the camp, no sign of life, just the two ships standing bright in the sunlight. Wayne unbuckled himself and took one step over to the radio. It was already tuned to the international call-band. He picked up the microphone and said in a flat voice: 'This is Captain Wayne calling Colonel Byelinsky. This is Captain Wayne, N.A.U., calling the Siberian expedition. Come in, come in, Siberia.'

The set hummed and crackled. Collie shook his head to clear it, he was still half deafened by the rocket noise, and freed himself. When he stood up, he was trembling uncontrollably. Strange, the calm which had fallen on Wayne.

'Byelinsky.' Collie jumped as the voice crackled out of the loudspeaker. Almost, he could see the man, square-built, erect, squinting across at the newcomer. He didn't think the Siberian would show dismay. The same cool smile, the same tone of aloof humor, yes, that would be his way of dying.

'You have three of our personnel imprisoned,' said Wayne. 'Release them at once, and we can negotiate.'

'We have only two, I fear,' replied Byelinsky. 'Ivanovitch was killed aiding Collingwood's escape.'

Misha dead, Misha of the boisterous mirth and the unspoken comradeship, he was down with dust in his mouth and would never laugh again: Collie felt a stinging in his eyes.

'Well,' said Wayne coldly. 'Let the others go.'

'I have no mind to do so,' answered Byelinsky, without rancor. 'They are useful hostages.'

'If you don't,' said Wayne, 'we will destroy you.'

'With what?' asked the colonel. 'I know you haven't any artillery. We need only sit here and wait for our own assault party to return. If you are wise, it is you who will ask for terms.'

Wayne's face and voice were like a speaking mask. Byelinsky might have been some piece of mechanism that wasn't functioning properly. 'I do not intend to bandy words,' he said. 'You will get no chance to lift off the ground. You know who I am. You have exactly one minute to surrender.'

There was no response. Wayne sighed and took the resonator in his hands. 'Collie,' he asked, 'where is their brig?'

'Right there,' pointed the hillman. 'In the waist o' that ship, unless they've been moved.'

'That's a chance we'll have to take,' said Wayne. He flipped a switch, and the resonator hummed as it began to warm up.

The thought of Lois wiped out by that beam was too much for a mind to hold. Collie rejected it with a convulsive movement of his hands.

An airlock door opened and three suited figures stood waiting for the ladder to reach ground. One held a superbazooka.

The resonator glowed, somewhere in its tube.

'Those birds can hole us if they get a chance,' said Collie.

'I know,' said Wayne. He turned back to the radio. 'Byelinsky?'

'Yes?'

'Your time is up. I think. Do you wish to surrender?'

'No.'

'Goodbye, Byelinsky,' said Wayne, gently and with a note of regret.

He went back to the viewport and sighted along the resonator. 'I've only used this once before,' he said. 'It was an ugly sight. I had nightmares for years. Well –'

He turned a dial, focusing. Then he tripped a switch.

One of the men on the ladder went up in a huge crack of fire and smoke. Another tumbled to the ground, his helmet shattered by the explosion of his brain. The third tried to retreat. It was horribly like a singed moth crawling from a flame. Wayne stamped him into scattering smoke.

Flame began to jet from that ship. It must have been warming up. Wayne refocused and played his invisible beam over it. The ship lay there, still fuming, till there was a haze of dust and ice in the air. There was no one alive to turn off the motors.

Byelinsky's voice stammered from the receiver: 'You criminal – favorable mutants – I have your people hostage, I tell you! They will die if –'

'You are the one who will die,' said Wayne. 'We haven't enough men to board your vessel. Will you come out and surrender?'

Proudly. 'No.'

Wayne scythed the other ship, passing over the midsection. Then there was silence. The Martian wind scattered the smoke which had been men.

18

The cutting torch hissed into extinction. For a moment the steel door was too hot to touch. Then Collie had wrapped his hand in a cloth and flung it open. 'Lois,' he whispered. He had thought to plunge in and grasp her to him, but now when she stood there in O'Neill's arms, looking at him with a dazed kind of wonder, his hands fell to his sides. 'I'm glad you're alive,' he said.

The Irishman was choking in the greasy reek that swirled through the ship. 'Let's get the hell out of here,' he mumbled. 'I think I'm going to be sick. What devil's gadget were you after using?'

'Ah don't know,' said Gammony, picking up his torch. 'An' Ah don' think Ah want to know, neither.'

They clambered into airsuits and made their way outside. Lois laid a hand on Collie's arm. 'So you got through,' she said. 'That was a wonderful thing you did.'

'Uh, well, that's all past.' He shifted on his feet, uncertainly. The hard sunlight struck through the girl's helmet and he couldn't take his eyes off her face. 'You're alive an' well, that's the main thing.'

'So it's captured the ships you have, eh?' O'Neill looked around the camp. 'Quite a stroke. With their fuel and supplies and equipment, our own Mars project is a long way ahead at one jump. We can install a lot of their stuff right in our own camp,

171

and the rest can wait here for the next expedition to take.' He frowned. 'But what about that war party that went out?'

'They'll be back,' said Collie, 'but they ain't got a chance. We'll ambush 'em a few miles out in the hills. I think they'll surrender. I hope so – wouldn't be fun blowin' 'em up.' There had only been two survivors of Byelinsky's group, men who happened to be near the cell. They were locked up now themselves, and one was weeping.

'I figger any pris'ners we take, we can seal inside a disabled ship,' went on Collie. 'They'll have food an' air, but no tools. Won't hurt 'em to wait here till the next American boat comes.'

O'Neill's gaunt melancholy face broke into a grin. 'With this information, the Union is bound to get going on the Mars project,' he said. 'And as the late colonel remarked, one colony can hold the entire planet if need be. Though I think the Khan will be a lot less obstreperous when he learns what's happened. Faith, this is one time things do end right!'

'No,' said Lois. 'They haven't ended. They've just begun.'

Her gloved hand stole into O'Neill's, and she smiled up at him. 'Just begun,' she repeated.

The Irishman looked foolish and happy. He turned to Collie. 'How about being my best man when we get back to Earth?' he asked.

'Best man!' He couldn't realize it. The lightning hit too swiftly.

'Uh-huh. When we were locked up in there, with nothing much to hope for – well, she said yes.'

'The seventy-seventh proposal, it was,' she laughed. Her eyes were warm on O'Neill.

'Um, uh, well,' said Collie. He had to clear his throat a couple of times. 'Sure, thanks, I'd like to be best man. We'll throw you a real weddin'. An', an', congratulations.'

He muttered some excuse and turned around and walked off. There was work to do around camp, but he had to get away by himself and think.

He found a rock high over the valley and sat down and looked across the desert. It was quiet and lonely up here. There was something big about this landscape.

They will change their minds, women, he thought. *It happens. Or mebbe she was only usin' me to make him jealous.*

There'll be others, he told himself. *It was just that she was the only woman on the planet.*

He guessed that it would take a year or so before he got himself to really believing that.

Well, what the devil. A year wasn't so long, when you had a whole future to shape. There was Earth, wide and fair and green, and there was Mars where a man could grow up along with a whole new race of humankind. Yes, he thought, in more than one sense he was lucky.

So – Collie shrugged. So there was work to do. Right now, for instance. He got up and went down the slope toward the ships. The children of fortune were already busy there.

As he descended, the sky seemed to grow darker, so that he could more clearly discern the few bright stars. But the sun was still high, and it filled the valley with light.

Epilogue

Orna of Nildo was a courteous host who wished his guest to see all the sights. Ganymede didn't have many, but the midnight sky was worth a good deal else. He helped Danivar into flexarmor; he himself needed only put on a coat and facial mask. They floated up the gravity shaft together, out the retention field of the turret doorway, and stood on the surface.

Danivar had of course seen pictures and descriptions of the view. But reality snatched the breath from him. Jupiter at full phase was a vast amber shield, banded with violet, pale red, and a hundred subtler hues. Low above the horizon, it turned crags and scarps into gold, the frozen lake beneath into a chalice that brimmed with radiance. No stars were visible near the giant planet, and few enough on the opposite side of the sky; but such as there were flashed like strewn diamonds. Somehow the quietness was not total; as if with sharper ears one could hear the thin cold singing of the stars.

After a very long while, Danivar glanced at the thermometer on his wrist. The light was more than enough to read by, though the metal sparkled frostily. 'A hundred below.' He knew his remark was inane, but he chose it to offset that which surrounded him as a jewel shines best on a black background. 'I expected worse.'

'Our new fusion plants down under the crust are warming the environment up faster than most people realize,' said Orna. 'Of course, we'll need at least another century before Ganymede is at all comfortable, and I'll be quite an old man, I expect, before we can call our task finished. You don't convert a moon as big as a small planet overnight. Nonetheless, I can remember when I was a boy, we hadn't even produced a hydrosphere, let alone air.'

As if the hugeness around had touched his pride, he added

apologetically, 'I don't suppose this impresses you much, you being from the richest planet in the System.' He raised an arm. The tawny chill light seemed to drip from his glove. 'Look, there's your home, over near Leo. That green star.'

'On the contrary,' said Danivar, 'we Martians are the ones who can most respect a project like yours. How do you think our own world was built?'

'But that was so long ago.'

'We've never forgotten.'

They fell silent again. Not that their conversation had been in so many words. A gesture, a syllable, the total context of the night and themselves, were enough for such brains. Physically they were dissimilar, for the race still tended to make somatic adaptations to local conditions. But size and shape and metabolic requirements were the least important things about them.

The cold seemed to deepen. Danivar's body was protected by the flexarmor; his self was not. Orna saw him huddle the least bit and nodded: 'Would you like to go back inside?'

'No, thank you. Not yet.' Danivar turned to face the king planet. Its light flooded his eyes, so that for a moment he was sinking into Jupiter, becoming a part thereof, and thus a part of the entire cosmos. And this, far more than any philosophic creativity meeting, was the reason he had traveled here.

When he drew his attention back, he felt that sadness which is the price of transcendence. He said, as if to himself, 'There was so much life there once.'

'What?' Orna stirred, restless. The sound of his feet on naked rock rang more loudly through the thin air than one might have expected.

'Earth.' Danivar's gaze sought the sky again, but he couldn't find the planet he named. 'I was there for a while several years ago, as esthetician of an archeological party.'

'Oh? I thought that was an exhausted field. How many millennia have you Martians been digging on Earth?'

'Much fewer than the Old Humans lived there. A million years hence, we may turn up flint arrowheads or ceramic vessels. The site I helped excavate wasn't that ancient, however. In fact, quite late, probably founded a bare century prior to the Final

War. Artifacts indicated it was inhabited afterward too, and that the last dwellers took part in the emigration to Mars.'

'You mean when the terrestrial biosphere collapsed?'

'Yes. That dates the site rather closely. We know from surviving records how narrow the escape was. If it had taken Alaric Wayne ten years longer to establish a self-sufficient terrestroid ecology on Mars, you and I would not be here now.'

'I've been taught that much. Also how the project in turn depended on settling the tribal quarrels of time peacefully, so that all Earth's resources could be devoted to the task. In the end, to save themselves, the Old Humans redeemed themselves.'

Danivar's smile was not gentle. 'I suspect a good deal of force and intrigue was involved in their reformation. There aren't any turning points in history, except those we arbitrarily choose long afterward. We look at the hopeful aspect, the relative few who were biologically fit and could be evacuated to Mars, and forget the long-drawn tragedy of the deformed who must be left behind to die. Nor was that first Martian settlement the genesis of modern hominid life. The effort to achieve genetic stability required millennia.' His eyes crossed the sawtoothed mountains and went on beyond his home world. 'So I do not blandly consider that all worked out for the best. Had it not been for that damned war and its aftermath, we might stand here amidst flowering gardens and know that our people had already reached the stars.'

'We would not exist,' said Orna prosaically.

Danivar laughed. 'True. The trend of events must ever seem toward the best, since it is toward the one observing the trend. And after all, I went to Earth to help excavate that site before it was buried under an impounded river, as part of the ecological restoration program. Earth too shall bloom.'

His tone dropped low. 'And yet,' he said, 'I cannot forget what we found in those ruins. Imagine. There I stood, in a desert more grim than any on Mercury, because Mercury is still decently barren whereas there a few primitive plants tried in their distorted fashion to live. And the wind blew around those old, old snags of walls, and the sunlight of Earth spilled over us with a horrible brilliant indifference.

'I held a box in my hand. A small box of some resistant alloy, not too badly corroded. When I opened it, I found a clutter of objects, coins, ornaments, keys, valuables of one sort or another, chiefly masculine. They included an oblong of stiff paper. One side had been a garish colored photograph, of which little remained, but the writing on the other side was decipherable yet. A mail communication, which the receiver had preserved.'

The shadow of a moon began to cross Jupiter's face. The night seemed to make an inaudible sound, as if the stones underfoot groaned with the gathering cold. Orna waited.

'I'd spent a few hours learning the ancient languages, of course,' said Danivar at last. 'Now I almost wish I hadn't. For I stood with the wind gibing at me, there on the old broken planet, and read what had been written. Not that it was anything so special,' he added hastily. 'But I've wondered about lingering auras. A hundred generations hence, when the sense of perception is fully developed, we may know.

'Anyhow! The message was to someone named Hugh Drummond, a masculine name. The point of origin was named St. Louis, Missouri, and the date was just prior to that recorded for the outbreak of the Final War. What it said was merely, *Darling, All's well. Do finish your business soon. I don't want to hustle you or anything, and of course your work is important, but the kids and I miss you so much. I can't help wishing you hadn't postponed that holiday we were going to take together, just by ourselves. Well, next year! All my love, Barbara.*'

'Isn't that the earliest personal letter ever found?' Orna asked. 'I never heard of your discovery before. We get rather parochial, I'm afraid, out on the frontier.'

'What a beautiful word that is,' Danivar mused. 'Frontier. And yet . . . I don't know. The ancestors survived, enough of them, and now we are pleased to call ourselves Homo Superior, but we'll never know what might have lived in our place.'

'A bit too late for that sort of speculation,' said Orna.

'Yes.' Danivar shivered. 'I think I would like to go back inside now.'

**In a future world of strangers,
the hunter and the hunted are one . . .**

ROGER ZELAZNY

Winner of 3 Nebula and 3 Hugo Awards

William Blackhorse Singer, the last Navajo tracker on a future earth, has stocked the Interstellar Life Institute with its most exotic creatures. But one of Singer's prizes preys upon his mind: a metamorph. The one-eyed shapeshifter Cat, whose home planet has been destroyed. Singer offers Cat freedom to help him defend Earth against a terrible predator, and Cat accepts. The price: permission to hunt the hunter. And the deadly game begins. In a fierce, global hunt, Singer flees his extra-sentient killer. And suddenly, he is pursuing not life, but the mysteries of his people, and the blinding vision of his own primeval spirit . . .

'Zelazny's best book since *Lord of Light*.' *Joe Haldeman.*
'The interweaving of old tales and futuristic adventures is genuinely moving . . .'
New York Times Book Review.
'The melting together of perceptions of the future and the past are brilliant, effective and moving.'
Vonda McIntyre.

SCIENCE FICTION   0 7221 9442 0   £1.95

Also available by Roger Zelazny in Sphere Science Fiction:

THE HAND OF OBERON   NINE PRINCES IN AMBER
MY NAME IS LEGION   THE GUNS OF AVALON
SIGN OF THE UNICORN   THE COURTS OF CHAOS
DAMNATION ALLEY

From one of Science Fiction's most acclaimed
writers comes an outstanding new edition to the
popular DORSAI series

LOST DORSAI

Gordon R. Dickson

WINNER OF THE NEBULA AWARD FOR THE BEST NOVELLA OF 1981

Revolution gripped the mighty kingdom of El Conde ..

As the gap between rich and poor yawned cavernously
wider, the massed ranks of the Naharese exploded
into bitter rebellion. Men who had been trained by the
galaxy's most famous warriors, the Dorsai, now took
up arms against them. And into this chaos were flung
a handful of noble Dorsai warriors, whose innate
honour bound them to secure El Conde from the
rebels. Their might was pitted against the most
impossible odds: but one of their number faced battle
first of another kind entirely, forced to grapple with a
sudden, terrifying loss of conviction in the ways of
warriorhood central to his whole existence . . .

SCIENCE FICTION   0 7221 30201   £1.95

TERROR FROM BEYOND THE STARS

THE QUEEN OF THE LEGION

Jack Williamson

From the innermost core of the Nebula they swarm
forth in their nightmarish hordes . . . Beware the
shadowflashers: terrible parasites who will ruthlessly
enslave your mind and body. They have already
captured AKKA, the great secret weapon. They have
killed the Keeper of the Peace . . . and they will stop at
nothing. Who now can stand between the human
race and ultimate destruction . . . ?

Jil Gyrel, courageous daughter of a lost Legion pilot,
has inherited her father's prescience and his uncanny
navigational gifts. She is the first to sense the inhuman
danger . . . but can the strength of this valiant girl
alone save the future of Mankind?

QUEEN OF THE LEGION is the fourth novel in the
classic LEGION OF SPACE series — a thrilling tale of a
battle against the most monstrous evil ever to emerge
from the treacherous regions of outer space.

SCIENCE FICTION   0 7221 9196 0   £1.95

A selection of bestsellers from SPHERE

FICTION

CHANGES	Danielle Steel	£1.95 ☐
FEVRE DREAM	George R. R. Martin	£2.25 ☐
LADY OF FORTUNE	Graham Masterton	£2.75 ☐
THE JUDAS CODE	Derek Lambert	£2.25 ☐
FIREFOX DOWN	Craig Thomas	£2.25 ☐

FILM & TV TIE-INS

THE DUNE STORYBOOK	Joan Vinge	£2.50 ☐
ONCE UPON A TIME IN AMERICA	Lee Hays	£1.75 ☐
MORGAN'S BOY	Alick Rowe	£1.95 ☐
MINDER – BACK AGAIN	Anthony Masters	£1.50 ☐

NON-FICTION

BACHELOR BOYS – THE YOUNG ONES' BOOK	Rik Mayall, Ben Elton & Lise Mayer	£2.95 ☐
THE COMPLETE HANDBOOK OF PREGNANCY	Wendy Rose-Neil	£5.95 ☐
THE STORY OF THE SHADOWS	Mike Read	£2.95 ☐
THE HYPOCHONDRIAC'S HANDBOOK	Dr. Lee Schreiner and Dr. George Thomas	£1.50☐

All Sphere books are available at your local bookshop or newsagent, or can be ordered direct from the publisher. Just tick the titles you want and fill in the form below.

Name_____

Address_____

_____

Write to Sphere Books, Cash Sales Department, P.O. Box 11, Falmouth, Cornwall TR10 9EN

Please enclose cheque or postal order to the value of the cover price plus:

UK: 55p for the first book, 22p for the second and 14p per copy for each additional book ordered to a maximum charge of £1.75.

OVERSEAS: £1.00 for the first book and 25p for each additional book.

BFPO & EIRE: 55p for the first book, 22p for the second book plus 14p per copy for the next 7 books, thereafter 8p per book.

Sphere Books reserve the right to show new retail prices on covers which may differ from those previously advertised in the text or elsewhere, and to increase postal rates in accordance with the PO.